Haute Mess:

Book 1
The Royal Griffen Hotel Mystery Series

Erica J Whelton

Publisher: Sunseri Design Publishing
Cover Designer: CJ Love – Pixel Squirrel
ISBN: 978-1-956069-51-8

Printed in the United States of America

To my mom for trying to teach me to sew!
I can still make a pillow but that's about it.

Chapter One

I stretched and looked out the window at the city skyline. It was just a speck in the distance.

"Good morning, Pippa!"

My dog twitched her oversized black and white ears, but she didn't move. She had never been a fan of mornings, even as a little pup.

It had been pouring rain the day I found her in an abandoned box in front of my shop. She looked up at me with her little bug eyes and too large for her head ears. I knew I couldn't just leave her there.

"Oh, you poor thing," I said, picking her up and holding her close.

She whimpered in my arms, burying herself into my coat.

"Let's get you dried and find you a little bit of kibble, Pippa."

The rest was history. We'd been inseparable since. She was my best friend and the only one who knew the real me. Everyone, and I mean everyone, thought I was this eccentric person. I liked that and did everything I could to keep that rumor going.

I swung my legs over the bed and padded my way over to my treadmill. As I pulled the clothing from it, I giggled. This was one of those odd secret things people would probably laugh about.

What's my secret? I was more able than everyone thought. I used my treadmill daily, keeping it covered in random things so if anyone came over, they would assume I didn't. Around most, I acted like a feeble old lady.

For some weird reason, this amused me.

I'd always been a little bit strange. As a child, I was the kid who lived in a hotel. But I loved the hotel, still do, but those early years it was full of secrets. The dumbwaiters had been removed in most units and covered up in others, but I would travel in them, listening to private conversations, and spying on unsuspecting guests.

The few times she'd catch me, my mother would get fierce with me.

"Dora Lee Griffen, you cannot be spying on people!" Then she'd whip me once and send me to my room. Thankfully, she'd only caught me a few times and I learned how to be even quieter.

The memory had me walking faster as I giggled.

The only thing I knew from a young age was that I loved to design clothing. I could spend hours picking fabrics, matching different textures and blending them into gowns, day dresses, or fancy coats. Whatever it was. I had finally opened my own shop. It was just down the block from my apartment.

After a thirty-minute walk, I headed to the kitchen to fill Pippa's bowl with kibble and give her fresh water.

"Okay, Pip, I'm going to hop in the shower."

Post shower, I stood in front of my extra-large mirror looking at my reflection. I was dressed in a black and white checked tunic that came just below my knees. On a taller person it probably hit at the waist, but oh well. I wore black leggings underneath with a mustard yellow open cardigan over the tunic, my little slip-on Mary Jane shoes, and black socks.

"Whatcha think, Miss Pippa?" I asked my faithful companion.

She blinked, then did her Pippa head tilt. Her too large ears flopped over when she did. The ears are what first caught my eye when she was just an abandoned pup in a box. Her ears were almost bigger than she was back then. For the most part, she'd grown into them, but they were still eye-catchingly large.

"I'll take that as a nod of approval."

I grabbed my purse and keys. Pippa hopped and yipped at me, excited to go to the shop. She loved people watching in the front window and getting attention from the few shoppers that actually came in. Though those were becoming fewer and fewer with each passing day.

"Maybe I should retire?" I thought it numerous times a day, but as the fabrics were sewn together, buttons, zips, and clasps added and a new outfit emerged, I knew I couldn't quit yet. Not as long as this mind and these hands still worked.

I clipped Pippa's leash to her pink plaid collar, custom made with her name on it in rhinestones. Her little pink toenails clicked happily along the smooth marble tiles to the front door.

We stepped out of the penthouse of Royal Griffen Hotel, though it hadn't been a hotel in years, not since my daddy passed away in the seventies. The new owners turned it into luxury apartments, but I was part of the deal. I got to keep the south facing penthouse, the one my family called home since before I was born.

I stepped into the beautiful hallway to the smell of fresh flowers that were always placed on the table outside the elevator by the apartment staff. That was another detail I had insisted on. There must be fresh flowers in all hallways and in all common areas. That was something my mother had always ensured, even if she had to go out to the fields and cut them herself.

I hit the down button and waited. Pippa bounced from side to side.

"Almost here."

She tilted her head, then went back to bouncing from side to side.

The elevator clunked into place then the soft chime sounded its arrival.

"Oh!" I jumped slightly as the doors slid open to reveal two young men in what appeared to be a tense discussion. This was the top floor, so it normally came to this floor empty.

They quieted when they saw me.

"Are you getting off or going down?" I asked them.

"Hi Miss Dora. We're going down. We got on going the wrong direction." One of the young men shouted.

I had met him before. I'd led him to believe I was going deaf. It was another fun game I played with myself that nobody else knew I played. I loved being old.

People underestimated us, walked past us, and expected our bodies to be falling apart. I was fit as a fiddle and sharp as a tack, but that's not what people around me thought. I didn't mind keeping the stereotype going, if only to make life a little more fun for myself.

"Thank you, Evan," I said to him. "Come along, Miss Pippa."

"It's Ethan, Miss Dora Lee," he said.

"Of course. Thank you, Eric." I fought the urge to giggle.

He simply smiled, but his friend looked annoyed and crossed his arms over his chest. I noted his outfit as I shuffled into the elevator. Expensive. Well-tailored. The jacket was definitely from Viola's spring collection two years ago. I recognized the distinctive cut and the signature buttons she used that season. The boy had good taste, I'd give him that.

I just stared straight ahead as the doors closed.

Ethan turned to his friend, lowering his voice. "Milo, you need to reconsider."

"We can't talk about this now," Milo said quietly, nodding in my direction.

"She can't hear a thing unless you shout," Ethan said. "Watch. I'm going to kick your dog."

I laughed on the inside, but didn't even flinch. Pippa on the other hand turned to face him. She was a smart little thing. Ethan was a sweet boy and I knew it wasn't real.

"I'm going to kidnap your dog and eat her for dinner," Milo said.

Again, I didn't react even though I wanted to punch Milo square in his jaw. I just had a bad feeling about that boy. He had a darkness in him that was missing from his friend, an anger that simmered just below the surface.

"Okay, fine. I believe you. So, what's next then?" Milo asked.

"The current models aren't working with the designs. We need to finish those pieces and then rebook new models."

"They've been booked through their agents, contracts signed. What do I tell them?"

"Just don't say anything. Just sign new ones."

"Ethan, we can't just ghost them. They have contracts."

"With a clause in it. Book new models."

"We'll never be able to hit the deadline. The show is in a week."

"Models are a dime a dozen in this town. We'll be fine," Ethan said.

"But to find ones that meet the size requirements in that timeframe."

This all caught my attention as I was in the fashion design business and hadn't realized that Ethan was as well. I really had to fight the urge now to let them know I was listening.

"Money has already changed hands and everything is set up. We just need to finish the work."

"I think you're a dreamer with unrealistic goals. This deadline is tight."

"It will be fine. You worry too much."

We hit the bottom floor and the elevator opened. Pippa and the boys exited, but I stood firm pretending not to notice.

"Miss Dora Lee ... um ... we reached the bottom floor," Ethan said, just as the elevator doors closed. Once the door was closed and I was out of sight, I pushed a button to go back up. Another funny thing I liked to do. Acting confused. I laughed for the entire ride up and then back down.

Pippa knew the routine and would stay in the lobby waiting for me.

The doors, once again, opened at the lobby.

"Oh, my! What happened to me?" I asked as I got off this time. "Where is my little Pippa? Pippa, where are you?"

That's when I saw Ethan rush over. His friend, Milo, was red in the face. If he was a cartoon, smoke would be coming from his ears.

"I have her, Miss Dora Lee. She's safe," Ethan said, bringing her over. He handed me her pink leash.

"Thank you so much, Ian."

"Can I walk you to your shop?" he asked.

"Oh, that would be lovely." I took his arm. "Come along, Pippa."

Milo let out a heavy sigh as he shuffled behind us. Ethan chatted the entire block to my shop, talking about the weather, the neighborhood, nothing of consequence. But I listened to his tone, watched how he carried himself. Confident. Charming. Used to getting his way.

"Well thank you so much, dear." I pulled my coin purse from my purse, fishing around for just the right coin. "Here. For your troubles." I handed him a quarter.

"Um, oh, no thank you. I can't take this," Ethan said, an amazed smile on his face. "You keep it."

"I insist. Buy yourself a soda." I knew full well a soda didn't cost a quarter any longer, but it gave me a little giggle to think about.

He took it, flipping it in his hand, sharing an amused glance with Milo.

"Thank you. Have a good day."

"You too, boys!" I waved after them, then unlocked the shop and flipped on the lights. The colorful creations that welcomed me in had my heart skipping a beat. The mannequins dressed in my clothing, the racks full of yet to be sold items, and the alterations area with its piles of fabric and spools of thread waiting to become something beautiful.

My ancient sewing machines were also waiting. I had patterns and swatches that I was dying to try out, but without people to buy, what was the point?

I bent down to unclip Pippa's leash and she immediately trotted over to her sleeping spot in the display window. I watched her climb onto her fluffy pink bed, do three turns, dig a little, then turn three more times before settling.

I shook my head as I laughed. She'd come a long way from that soaking wet puppy to the spoiled pooch six years later.

As I stood there watching her, someone on the street stopped to look in the shop window. She laughed when she saw Pippa there, but then she took a long look at the two dresses on display.

One was a long maxi style dress with blue and creamy white stripes running vertically. The fabric was a soft cotton. It was perfect for summer. I imagined a wide brim hat and strappy sandals, a straw tote bag full of picnic supplies.

The other was a red and black windowpane patterned dress with a peter pan collar. The kids today would call it retro but it was the first style of dress I learned to sew and was my favorite. The pattern gave it a more modern feel that I hoped would appeal to today's market.

She looked at the sign then pushed the door open.

I turned with a smile to greet her. "Hello. Welcome to Dora Lee's. I'm Miss Dora Lee. Are you looking for something specific?"

"I just love the two in the window and thought I would have a look around."

"Wonderful. All items are hand-sewn by me and if you like one, but don't see your size, I can make one specifically for you. I also do custom work."

"Thank you. I'll let you know."

With that she looked around. I didn't want to stare so I busied myself with rearranging some in-store displays and trying to decide if I should add another outfit to the window. Perhaps a jumper that I'd finished recently or maybe add different accessories?

Peeking over at the young lady who'd come in, she had a few items in her hand. I sighed with relief. I hadn't sold much lately.

I used to be a top designer. Now, I owned a dusty shop with one customer a week, if I was lucky. She was my second this week, so it was a good week.

Thank goodness for my inheritance and my past earnings. It was keeping me going.

"Do you have a dressing room?"

"Oh, yes of course." I gestured to the three stalls with curtains. "Just let me know if you need any assistance with zippers or snaps."

She nodded.

I fidgeted around as I waited. Five minutes or so passed before she came out.

"These are beautiful. I'll take these two."

"Wonderful and good choices. I'll ring you up." I was awful at small talk so I quickly finished her transaction and she was on her way.

Once she was gone, I busied myself around the shop with cleaning, rearranging and creating new displays. Then I set out a pattern, cutting the fabric, before getting to work.

It was hours later before I walked to the window to check on Pippa. She yawned and looked up at me, giving a slight wag of her tail.

"You know you are too young to be this lazy."

She laid her head back down.

Movement to the right caught my eye. It was that kid, Milo, that I'd seen earlier with Ethan. He was running away from Royal Griffen Hotel dressed in gym clothes. I glanced at the clock. Just after two o'clock. I noted it automatically, the way I'd trained myself to notice details. That same jacket from Viola's collection, the distinctive buttons catching the light even from here. The boy was devoted to her designs.

I shrugged when he rounded the corner on West Avenue.

Roughly an hour later, it was time to call it a day.

"This is what I love about running my own business, Pippa. I can set my own hours," I said as I clipped the leash to her collar.

I locked up and as we started to walk the block home, a police car whizzed by followed by another. Then an ambulance soon followed.

I looked around to see if anyone was paying attention to me. They weren't, so I changed my pace from my usual shuffle to the quicker pace I used on the treadmill. I arrived to find that many of the building's residents were standing on the street.

There were murmurs about a death, but I had no idea who and I wanted to know.

I ignored what was going on and shuffled my way into the lobby.

"Ma'am, you need to wait outside," an officer said.

Without even stopping or acknowledging him, I kept walking.

"Ma'am... ma'am?" He continued to say.

"That's Miss Dora Lee. She's old and can't hear well," Walter, the doorman, said. He caught my eye for just a moment, and I saw the hint of a smile. Walter had worked here for fifteen years. He knew exactly what I was doing.

"Yeah, she's harmless. Came with the building," the apartment manager, Chelsea, said with a slight smirk.

"Fine." The officer waved to some of the other officers before turning back to the crowd, letting me go on my merry way. I loved being underestimated.

I got to the elevator and saw the main scene appeared to be in our onsite gym.

"Oh dear!" I said. "What is all this about?"

"Um, ma'am, you aren't supposed to be over here."

"I live here and I have rights."

"I understand, but this is a crime scene," the young female officer explained. "You should go either to your apartment or wait on the street with the others."

"My family built this hotel ... er, apartments! I have rights, you know. Rights!" I shouted and acted offended. "You can't tell me where to go."

"Actually, I can, and right now, you cannot be contaminating my crime scene," she said, looking around. "Jones? Where is that guy?"

With her distracted, I ducked under the crime scene tape and made my way to the gym door. From here, I could see them in the sauna area. There was a body under a cloth.

I couldn't hear everything that was being said, but I heard something about the latch failing and him getting overheated.

That didn't seem likely as it didn't get that hot in there. Warm and steamy, yes, but unless he had a medical condition, he should have been able to handle it. Plus, there was an emergency latch inside the sauna if the main one failed.

Suddenly there was a hand on my shoulder. I turned to find the angry face of the female officer.

"I told you not to come in here."

"Unhand me! I'm an old lady and fragile." I turned. "If you hurt me, I will sue you and everyone at city hall!"

Pippa began yipping at my side. All eyes in the place turned. I could hear Chelsea snickering.

"Just ... um, just please stand back here," she stammered as a red blush crept across her face.

"Oh, well ... okay then." I took a few steps back and ducked under the crime scene tape. "Better?"

"Yes, thank you." She started to walk away.

"Oh, dear, may I ask you a question?"

"Um, sure."

"What is your name?"

"My name? Keller. Detective Keller."

"Nice to meet you. I'm Miss Dora Lee Griffen. My parents were the original owners of this hotel, now apartment complex."

"Um, okay. Should that mean something?"

"Just to say that I know everything about this building and about everyone in it, or at least I know them. If you have any questions, I am happy to assist."

That last part might not be as true as it used to be. People were much more private than they used to be. Plus, I couldn't access all the dumbwaiters any longer so I couldn't go in and out of the apartments like I used to.

"I'll keep that in mind."

She went back to work without another look at me.

"Ethan! Ethan!" A voice yelled. As the figure came into view, it was Milo, Ethan's friend from earlier. He was dressed now in different clothes, no longer in his running gear. Still Viola's designs though. He had tears streaming down his face.

Officers stopped him.

"I have to get in there. That's my friend!"

"There's nothing you can do, son."

His shoulders slumped and he fell to the ground. A raw, painful wail came from his depths. Everyone in the lobby and gym area turned to watch him, then immediately went back to work on the scene.

I waited patiently watching it all, looking for anything that looked out of place or that the police might miss. Ethan was a sweet boy, young, ambitious, and from what I could tell, healthy. After an hour, Pippa was getting fidgety and likely wanted to go for her evening walk, so we left.

I gave one last look back just in time to see Milo watching us leave. His tears had long since dried up and he was now just sitting on one of the benches near the elevator, his face blank.

Not grieving anymore. Just watching.

Calculating.

Chapter Two

The good thing about being my age, you don't need as much sleep. I was wide awake at 3 am. Looking over, Pippa didn't move.

Now would be the perfect time for me to go snoop around the gym area.

Some might wonder why a seventy-eight-year-old woman would care about the death of a neighbor she barely knew. The truth was, I'd spent my whole life observing people, noticing details, solving puzzles in fabric and design. A murder in my own building was just another puzzle. And besides, my days had become rather predictable lately. Shop, home, shop, home. This was interesting.

I pulled on tennis shoes and pulled an oversized cardigan over my nightgown. I'm sure I would look like a nutty old lady wandering around half dressed like this. But that was the point. Out in the hallway, I paused at the elevator. If I pushed the button to go down, it would alert the front desk. It wasn't unusual for me to creep around at this time of night. I liked to keep tabs on the comings and goings. I'd always been too nosy for my own good.

But this time, I really didn't want anyone to see me.

Being on the tenth floor made the stairs difficult, but not impossible for me. I'd done it before, many times. I made my way down quietly. Between the seventh and eighth floor, I heard voices so I froze in place.

Television. Edgar Plowman must be awake. He was another early bird like me. He was often up watching TV. We sometimes ran into each other at the coffee house across the street.

When I reached five, I paused here thinking maybe I should try to check out Ethan's apartment. What would I be looking for there? The murder didn't take place there so I wouldn't know what clues to look for. The only thing I might learn was more about who he was, but I didn't care about that. I wanted to know about the murder.

Reaching the bottom floor, I pushed the door open quietly. It was just down the hall from the gym and sauna, and far enough from the reception desk and office that the night manager shouldn't be able to see me.

Even though this was no longer a hotel, they always had someone available for maintenance emergencies. Knowing Jerry, the night manager, he was watching television and dozing off in the office. He would never see me.

The crime tape was gone, but there were still smudges where the police had taken fingerprints and other DNA samples, at least I assumed. I examined a few of the spots but couldn't tell a thing from them. Even if I knew how to collect fingerprints, they were likely damaged from the officers' work.

I went into the sauna. The door looked to have been pried open with a crowbar or other such tool. The wood paneling was splintered and the metal frame twisted. Since I heard he'd been locked in and the latch failed, I assumed this is how they were able to get to him.

Inside the sauna, there was no blood, no sign of a fight or struggle.

Curious.

I sat on the bench and looked around the room. I hadn't been in here in years, not since I was in my twenties. It hadn't changed much.

Sitting here I tried to imagine what it would be like locked in and dying. A full body chill ran through me. Not a happy thought.

If I were stuck in here, I would have tried to claw my way out. With that thought, I went to examine the inside frame of the sauna. Sure enough there were scratch marks on the wall. It looked like they were confined to right around where the inside knob would be, if the door hadn't been ripped off by the rescue team.

I stared at them, trying to decide if this was a clue or just expected, sighing as I decided that it wasn't enough. It was expected, unless he'd been killed before realizing he was locked in.

With no sign or clue to be found, I headed back upstairs. This time I just took the elevator. Even if Jerry heard me, I would be upstairs long before he came out of the office.

When I got back to my apartment, I started my normal morning routine including walking two miles on my treadmill and ending with adding kibble to Pippa's bowl.

She finally stretched to come over and eat.

Once she was done eating, it was time to head out. Today was Wednesday which meant we would make a stop at the diner. It was our routine.

The bell over the door chimed as we walked in. Martin was in his place at the counter. He nodded in my direction.

"Mornin', Miss Dora Lee," Annie, the longtime waitress said. "And good morning, Miss Pippa!"

Pippa wagged her tail then hopped into our usual booth. Annie deposited a coffee mug in front of me, then filled it to the brim.

"I heard about that kid. Shame. Did you know him?"

"Not well. Just bumped into him here and there. He seemed like a sweet kid."

Martin turned slightly, making a gruff sound, then turned back to his platter of food. That was Martin, but it sounded like he agreed with me.

"The usual, hun?" Annie asked.

"Yes, thank you, Annie dear."

"Comin' right up."

I looked out the window. From here I had a nice view of the Royal Griffen Hotel. It was a gorgeous building with its granite and sandstone exterior and pointed archways on the windows and doors. Its age was showing, but in its prime, it was stunning. I had the picture of my parents standing proudly in front of it at the ribbon cutting. My mother's round belly showed that I would soon join them in the hotel business.

Little did they know, I would take a different career. I started sewing simple patterns by the time I was six and making all my own clothing as well as my mother's by the time I was eight. People started asking me to make them items and the rest was history.

But despite that, I loved that old building. It was my only home and my favorite place in the world to be. From all the secrets I'd overheard to all the people I'd met over the years, it had over seventy years worth of memories for me.

"Here you are, ladies." Annie set my wheat toast and two eggs over medium in front of me and a plate of scrambled eggs with a small piece of bacon in front of Pippa. She topped off my coffee. "Enjoy."

I watched Pippa dig into her treat, bacon first.

I smiled as I added a dash of salt and pepper to my eggs and slathered the bread with homemade strawberry jam.

As we were wrapping up our meal, a familiar figure came in. He was on his cell phone and speaking loudly. It almost startled me as it broke the usual diner sounds, causing the dozen or so people in the diner to stare at the intruder.

It was Milo, Ethan's annoying friend.

"No, no. I don't care. He is gone and we have to push things back. I don't care what it costs." He walked to the counter. "Black coffee." He snapped at Annie.

She stared at him but then turned to grab it as he continued to argue with the person on the phone. He seemed over his heartbreak from yesterday. His outfit today appeared to be another of Viola's. The boy had a style and he stuck with it.

My style changed all the time, and not always with the times. Today I was wearing a shift dress with an avocado and burnt orange daisy pattern with black tights and combat boots. Over the dress, I wore a cable knit black open front sweater. I loved it.

Annie set the coffee in front of Milo. He tapped his card, then as he turned to leave, he saw me for the first time. He froze in place as our eyes locked, but he recovered quickly and continued out the door.

"That one is a strange kid," Annie said, coming over to drop my bill.

"You know him?"

"Comes in here a few times a week. Always on the phone. It's the same routine. Rude." She shook her head. "Never says thank you, never tips. Just barks his order and leaves."

I watched through the window as Milo disappeared down the street, still on his phone, still agitated. Annie's words echoed in my head. Rude. Always the same routine. Always on the phone.

Who did Milo talk to? Who was in his ear?

The boy wore Viola's designs exclusively. That level of devotion to a single designer usually meant more than just appreciation for the aesthetic. It meant a relationship. Connection. Perhaps even mentorship.

Viola knew everyone in the menswear world. If Milo was a customer, she'd know him. And knowing Viola, she'd have opinions about him, about Ethan, about their partnership.

I needed to hear those opinions.

Viola. I'd need to talk to Viola.

We'd known each other for over forty years, since we were both clawing our way up in the fashion world. We met on the runways and at various shows, always circling each other like chess players sizing up the competition.

People who didn't know us well called us friends. People in the industry knew better. We were rivals who'd learned to coexist. Competitors who'd developed a working relationship because it was smarter to keep tabs on each other than to pretend the other didn't exist.

She'd gone into menswear when her husband insisted, building an empire out of necessity while I'd stayed in women's fashion. Different territories, which made the arrangement easier. But I'd never quite trusted her, and I suspected the feeling was mutual. There was something calculating in the way she watched people, the way she asked questions that seemed innocent but gathered information like a spider collecting flies.

Still, she knew everyone in the industry. She heard things. And if Milo was wearing her designs exclusively, she'd have opinions about him. Viola always had opinions.

Back at the shop, I waited until mid-afternoon when I knew Viola would be between appointments. She was always easier to reach in that sweet spot after lunch meetings but before evening obligations.

I dialed her number on my old landline phone.

"Hello."

"Hi, Vi. It's Dora Lee."

"Oh, hey Dora Lee. How's it going?" Her voice was warm, friendly. Viola was always good at that. Making you feel like she genuinely cared, right up until she didn't. "Good. Do you have time for dinner tonight?"

"Not tonight, but I could meet you tomorrow," she said.

"Okay, tomorrow at the diner."

"You and that diner." There was affection in her voice, but also something else. Amusement, maybe. Like she found my attachment to the place charmingly provincial. "You love the diner too."

"True. Okay, diner tomorrow at six?"

"Yes. See you then."

"Oh, before you go," Viola said. "I heard about that designer in your building. Ethan Kemper. Terrible thing."

"You knew him?"

"Not personally, but I knew of him. Everyone in the industry did. He was getting a lot of attention." She paused. "His partner, Milo Savage, is actually one of my best customers. Sweet boy. Very talented, but always seemed a bit overshadowed."

Perfect. I kept my voice light, casually interested. "You know Milo?"

Let her talk. Let her tell me everything.

"Oh yes. He's been buying my pieces for years. We've talked quite a bit at trunk shows and studio visits. He's got a good eye for design, very technically skilled. More than Ethan, actually, though Ethan got all the glory." She sighed. "I've seen it happen so many times in this industry. The flashy one gets the attention while the one doing the actual work stays invisible."

"That must be frustrating for him."

"I'm sure it is. Though he never complained to me. Very professional. But you could see it, you know? That frustration simmering underneath." Another pause. "Why do you ask? Are you investigating or something?"

"Me? No. Just curious. He lives in my building."

"Hmm." She didn't sound entirely convinced. "Well, if you want to know more about their dynamic, I'm happy to share what I know tomorrow. I've watched Milo grow as a designer over the years. He deserved better than being Ethan's shadow."

After we hung up, I sat there holding the phone, thinking about what Viola had said. She knew Milo well. Had watched him, talked to him, understood his frustrations.

He deserved better.

Those three words kept circling in my mind. Was it just observation? Or had she said something similar to Milo himself? Had she validated those feelings? Encouraged them?

I reminded myself to be careful tomorrow. Viola was useful, but she was also dangerous in her own way. The kind of person who collected secrets and used them when the timing was right.

Keep your friends close and your enemies closer. That's how we'd survived forty years of knowing each other.

Tomorrow at dinner, I'd learn more. And I'd be very careful about what I revealed in return.

Chapter Three

As I was leaving for work, I noticed there was a growing memorial of flowers, cards, and stuffed animals for Ethan. The pile had doubled in size overnight. Someone had added a poster-sized photo of him at what looked like a fashion show, his smile confident and bright.

I stopped to read a few of the cards. "Too young." "Taken too soon." "The fashion world has lost a star."

A young lady stood nearby, sobbing softly. I looked at her, then fished around in my purse for a tissue.

"Here." I thrust it at her.

"Thanks," she said, then dabbed her eyes. "Did you know him?"

"Um, not well. You know him?"

"Yes. We'd gone to school together. Madison Fashion Design Institute. He was brilliant. The next Mel Tanner."

"I know Mel. Good designer but awful man. Ethan was much sweeter than Mel."

She turned and looked at me for the first time. "Oh my gosh, you're Dora Lee Griffen. I... I am a huge fan. Huge. Look!" She whipped open her coat to reveal the dress underneath. It was one of my designs. "It was a gift from my mother. I could never afford your work on my own. It's my favorite." She ran a hand down the zig-zag black and white pattern.

"It looks beautiful on you." I studied her. "I might remember selling this to her. She had brought in your measurements."

"Yes, I was in Paris attending a runway show for Lawrence Jung."

"Oh, Jung does great pieces. Look at us, a relative who's who in fashion."

She gave a small laugh, the first genuine smile breaking through her tears. "I guess we are." She wiped her eyes. "You know, he has just moved to town."

"Jung?" I asked.

"Yes, he was going to be attending Ethan's first show. It was next week. Now Milo," she groaned. "He is canceling it. They are out all that money."

"So, you know Milo too?"

"Yeah, I'm his girlfriend. He is upstairs getting changed. We are meeting with Jung to discuss the changes to the show and Milo will be taking over Ethan's brand."

"Oh," I nodded and saved that bit of information for later. "Upstairs you say?"

"Yeah, he and Ethan were roommates."

The elevator chimed behind us and out strode the man in question. His eyes narrowed on me.

I took in his outfit in one quick glance. Charcoal gray suit, perfectly tailored. Single-breasted jacket with narrow lapels. The cut was distinctive, modern but with classic lines. I recognized it immediately as one of Viola's pieces from her spring collection two years ago. The same collection he'd been wearing yesterday at the diner.

It was interesting that he seemed to exclusively wear her designs.

"What are you doing here?" His voice was sharp, suspicious.

"She was just comforting me while I cried over Ethan," Ellie said. "Gave me a tissue. Thank you for that and this gorgeous dress. It really is my favorite."

"You are so welcome, dear. Oh my, I didn't catch your name."

"Ellie. Ellie Lands."

I took her hand, lightly squeezing it. "Nice to meet you, Ellie. Come along, Pippa."

Milo grabbed Ellie's arm, already steering her toward the door. "We're going to be late."

"I'll just be a second," Ellie said, pulling free. She turned back to me, lowering her voice. "Thank you again. For the tissue. For being kind."

"Of course, dear."

She hesitated, glancing back at Milo who stood by the door, arms crossed, radiating impatience. "Miss Dora Lee, can I ask you something?"

"Certainly."

"If someone you loved was changing, becoming someone you didn't recognize anymore, what would you do?"

I looked at this young woman, barely in her twenties, wearing my design and asking me for wisdom I wasn't sure I had.

"I'd ask myself if they're changing, or if I'm finally seeing who they really were all along."

She blinked, absorbing this. Then she nodded slowly. "Thank you. That's... that's helpful."

"Ellie!" Milo's voice cut across the lobby. "Now."

She flinched slightly, then straightened her shoulders. "I should go. It was lovely meeting you."

"You too, dear. Take care of yourself."

I watched her walk away, Milo's hand tight on her elbow as he guided her out the door. Through the glass, I could see him talking to her, his face angry, his gestures sharp. Ellie's shoulders were hunched, her head down.

Pippa pressed against my leg, whining softly.

"I know, girl. I don't like him either."

As Pippa and I started our walk to the shop, I nearly collided with Martin Plowman coming out of the diner across the street, a large cup in his weathered hands.

"Morning, Dora Lee," he said with his usual gruff nod.

"Good morning, Martin."

He gestured back toward the building with his cup. "Terrible business. That young man."

"It is."

"Heard it wasn't an accident." He took a sip of coffee. "Heard someone locked him in that sauna on purpose."

I kept my expression neutral. "Where did you hear that?"

"Chelsea. She was talking to that police officer. I was in the lobby picking up a package." He shook his head. "Who does something like that? Lock a man in to die?"

"Someone very angry."

"Or very calculating." Martin's eyes, usually half-lidded with boredom, were sharp now. "I've been thinking about it. That boy and his friend. They fought all the time. Heard them through the walls more than once. Yelling about money, about credit, about who did what work."

"You live on the fifth floor?"

"Right next door to them. 5B." He took another sip. "Week before he died, I heard them really going at it. Middle of the night. Something about 'I made you' and 'you'd be nothing without me.' Couldn't tell which one was saying what, but it was heated."

"Did you tell the police?"

"Nobody asked." He shrugged. "Figure they'll get around to questioning all of us eventually. Just thought you should know, since you live in the building too. We should all be watching out for each other."

"That's very true, Martin. Thank you."

He nodded and continued on his way, leaving me standing on the sidewalk with new information rattling around in my brain.

The morning air was crisp, and I could see my breath in little puffs. Fall was my favorite time of year in the city. The leaves were changing, people were bundling up in coats and scarves, and my shop windows could showcase my autumn collection.

Not that many people were buying, but a girl could dream.

As I unlocked the door and flipped on the lights, I mentally sorted through what I'd learned. Milo taking over Ethan's brand. The two of them were roommates, which meant Milo had constant access to Ethan. That fashion show they'd been arguing about was supposed to be next week. And now Martin's revelation about heated arguments over credit and who had made whom successful.

Pippa trotted to her window bed, doing her usual three turns and dig routine before settling in.

I moved around the shop, straightening displays that didn't need straightening, my hands busy while my brain worked. Ethan had wanted to push the show back. Milo had been furious about it. Now Ethan was dead and Milo was canceling the show anyway, but he was taking over the brand.

And he exclusively wore Viola's designs. That was worth noting. Tonight, at dinner, I'd ask her about him. She'd mentioned once that she had some loyal customers who bought multiple pieces. Maybe Milo was one of them.

I was arranging a display of scarves when the bell over the door chimed. A tall, slim young woman with striking red hair and a constellation of freckles across her nose walked in. She was gorgeous in that editorial way, all long limbs and sharp cheekbones.

"Good morning," I said, putting on my sweetest elderly shopkeeper voice. "Welcome to Dora Lee's."

"Hi," she said, glancing around. "I'm just looking, if that's okay?"

"Of course, dear. Take your time."

She moved through the racks slowly, touching fabrics here and there but not really looking at anything. Her mind was clearly elsewhere. I busied myself at the counter, watching her from the corner of my eye.

After a few minutes of aimless wandering, she drifted toward the window where Pippa was napping.

"Oh, what a cute dog," she said, her voice softening.

"That's Pippa. She loves the attention."

The young woman reached down to pet Pippa's head, and my dog, traitor that she was, immediately rolled over for belly rubs.

"She's precious." The girl smiled, but it didn't reach her eyes. "I'm Jamie, by the way."

"Miss Dora Lee. Lovely to meet you, Jamie."

She stood up, wrapping her arms around herself. "This is a beautiful shop. How long have you been here?"

"Oh, goodness, decades now. Right down the block from where I live at the Royal Griffen."

Her head snapped up at that. "The Royal Griffen? That's where..." She trailed off.

"Where that young man died, yes. Tragic. Just tragic." I shook my head sadly. "Did you know him?"

"Ethan? Yeah, I... I knew him." She turned back to the rack of dresses, fingers trailing over a blue silk number. "I modeled for him sometimes. Well, I used to."

"Used to?"

"He stopped booking me about six months ago. No explanation, just... stopped calling." She pulled out the blue dress, holding it up against herself without really seeing it. "I thought maybe I'd done something wrong, you know? Gained weight or said something stupid. But he never told me why."

"That must have been difficult."

"It was frustrating more than anything. I mean, I wasn't devastated or anything." She looked at the dress properly for the first time, her expression shifting. "Oh. This is beautiful."

"Would you like to try it on? I think it would look lovely on you."

She hesitated, then nodded. "Yeah. Yeah, I would."

I took the dress from her and led her to the dressing rooms. "Just let me know if you need help with the zipper."

While she changed, Pippa got up from her bed and wandered over, sitting at my feet and looking up at me with those big eyes.

"What?"

She tilted her head.

"She's a potential customer. Be nice."

Pippa's tail wagged, which I took as agreement.

When Jamie emerged from the dressing room, I caught my breath. The blue silk draped perfectly on her tall frame, the color making her red hair look even more vibrant and her skin luminous.

"Oh, honey. That's stunning."

She turned to look at herself in the full-length mirror, running her hands down the fabric. "It really is beautiful. The weight of it, the way it moves." She twisted slightly, watching the skirt swirl. "This is the kind of piece I used to dream about wearing to castings. Something that made me feel like I was already successful, you know?"

"I do know."

She met my eyes in the mirror. "Ethan used to tell me I'd be wearing designer pieces to every event once his brand took off. Said I'd be the face of his campaigns, that we'd do fashion week together." Her voice was bitter now. "Then he just... dropped me. Started using other girls. Never explained why."

"That must have hurt."

"It did. More than I wanted to admit." She smoothed the fabric over her hips. "He could be kind of a jerk sometimes, honestly. Super particular about everything. Nothing was ever good enough."

Pippa walked over to Jamie and sat at her feet, offering her paw.

Jamie laughed, a real laugh this time, and shook Pippa's paw. "Well, aren't you polite?"

"She knows how to make friends," I said.

Jamie bent down to scratch behind Pippa's ears. "I left flowers at the memorial this morning. Early, before anyone else was there. I wanted to pay my respects without everyone watching." She looked up at me. "Does that make me a hypocrite? Leaving flowers for someone who hurt me?"

"It makes you human, dear. People are complicated. We can be angry at someone and still grieve them."

"Yeah." She stood back up, looking at herself in the mirror again. "You know what's weird? I saw Milo yesterday, Ethan's business partner? He was already talking about taking over the brand. Like, the guy wasn't even cold yet and Milo's making plans." She shook her head. "This industry is ruthless."

"It sounds like you and Milo weren't close."

"We weren't. He always seemed... I don't know, resentful? Like he was angry all the time about something." She turned away from the mirror. "I should probably take this off. I can't really afford it right now anyway."

"You know what? Try this." I walked over to a rack and pulled out a simpler dress, still beautiful but in a less expensive fabric. "This one's on sale. Forty percent off."

It wasn't actually on sale, but I could tell she loved the blue dress and couldn't quite let go of the feeling it gave her.

She looked at the price tag, then back at the blue dress. "Can I think about it? Maybe come back in a few days?"

"Of course. I'll hold it for you if you'd like."

"Really?"

"Really."

Her smile was genuine this time. "Thank you. That's really kind." She went back into the dressing room to change.

When she came out, she placed the blue dress carefully on the counter. "I'll definitely be back. I just need to check my account, see what I can swing."

"Take your time, dear. It'll be here."

She headed for the door, then paused with her hand on the handle. "Miss Dora Lee? Do you think people can change? Like, really change who they are?"

It was the second time today someone had asked me about change.

"I think people show us who they are, bit by bit. Sometimes we just don't want to see it."

She nodded slowly. "That's what I was afraid of." Then she smiled sadly. "Thanks for letting me try on the dress. And for being nice. Not everyone is, especially to models who are on their way down."

"You're not on your way down, dear. You're just on your way to something different."

After she left, I stood at the window watching her walk down the street, shoulders hunched against a wind that wasn't there.

"Well, Pippa," I said, walking over to scratch behind her oversized ears. "This is getting more interesting by the minute."

She yawned in response.

I had a growing list of suspects now. Milo, who stood to gain Ethan's business and who wore nothing but Viola's designs. Lawrence Jung, the rival designer who'd just moved to town. And now Jamie Patton, the scorned model who'd left flowers at the memorial before anyone could see.

Dinner with Viola couldn't come soon enough.

Chapter Four

The diner was bustling when I arrived with Pippa at six o'clock sharp. I spotted Viola immediately. She was hard to miss with her platinum blonde hair styled in a sleek bob and her signature red lipstick. Even in her seventies, she looked like she'd just stepped off a runway.

"Dora Lee!" She waved from our usual booth near the back.

I shuffled over slowly, using my cane for effect even though I didn't really need it. A few regulars nodded hello as I passed. Viola watched my approach with those sharp eyes that missed nothing. I wondered what she was cataloging. My gait? My outfit? The fact that I'd suggested dinner when I usually avoided these meetings?

"Vi, darling. You look stunning as always."

"And you look like a kaleidoscope exploded in your closet," she said with a grin, eyeing my outfit. Today I'd chosen a purple and green paisley tunic over orange leggings with my favorite chunky turquoise necklace.

The comment could have been an insult from anyone else. From Viola, it was hard to tell. She had a way of delivering observations that kept you off balance, never quite sure if she was praising or critiquing.

"I'll take that as a compliment."

"As it was intended." She reached down to pet Pippa, who had already made herself comfortable under the table. "Hello, sweet girl."

At least Pippa trusted her. That was something.

Annie appeared with two coffee mugs and the pot. "Evening, ladies. The usual?"

"Please," we said in unison, then laughed. It was a practiced rhythm, this routine of ours. Forty years of dinners had created its own choreography.

"How's your mama doing, Annie?" I asked.

"Better, thanks for asking. The new medication is helping with her arthritis." Annie filled our cups to the brim. "I'll get your orders in."

Once she left, Viola leaned forward, wrapping her hands around her mug. I noticed how she did it. Casual. Relaxed. But her eyes were already working, already assessing.

Here we go. Let the game begin.

"So. That young designer in your building. Ethan Kemper. I heard about what happened."

Straight to it. No preamble. That was Viola. She didn't waste time on pleasantries when she wanted information.

"Terrible tragedy."

"You must have known him, living in the same building." Her eyes watched me carefully over the rim of her cup. "Were you close?"

I kept my expression neutral, took a sip of coffee. "Not really. Saw him in passing."

True, but not the whole truth. She'd know that. The question was whether she'd push.

"Still, it must be unsettling. A death in your building." She took a sip. "I heard it was an accident with the sauna?"

"That's what they're saying."

"But?" Viola tilted her head. "I know that tone, Dora Lee. You don't believe it was an accident."

Of course she'd caught that. Viola had always been good at reading people. It's what made her dangerous.

I shrugged, taking my time adding cream to my coffee. How much to reveal? How much to hold back? "The sauna doesn't get that hot. And there's an emergency latch inside."

"Curious." Viola's perfectly manicured nails tapped against her mug. A tell. She had those, everyone did. The tapping meant she was thinking, calculating. "Have you talked to the police? Told them your concerns?"

"They came by to take statements from everyone in the building."

"And did you mention these observations?"

There it was. The real question. What had I told the police? Viola wanted to know what information was already out there, already being investigated.

I kept my voice casual. "I answered their questions."

Not a lie, but not the whole truth either. Let her interpret that however she wanted.

Viola smiled slightly, as if I'd passed some kind of test. "Well, I suppose they'll figure it out. That's their job, after all." She paused. "Though I imagine someone as observant as you might have noticed things they missed."

"What makes you say that?"

"Oh, come on, Dora Lee. I've known you for forty years. You notice everything. It's what made you such a brilliant designer. That eye for detail." She leaned back as Annie arrived with our plates. "I'd bet you already have theories about what happened."

I focused on adjusting Pippa's dish of chicken, giving myself time to think. Viola was fishing. But why?
"I'd seen him around the building," I began, choosing my words carefully. "We never really spoke, not much more than a quick hello in the hallway or a polite nod in passing." My voice softened as I recalled that fateful morning. "But that morning, the one when he died. I did see him then. He seemed like a nice young man, from what little I knew." I let the statement hang in the air, hoping it was enough, neither too much nor too little, just as Viola would expect.

"Just him? Or was anyone with him?"

"His business partner was there. Milo Savage."

"Ah, Milo." Viola's expression brightened. But was it genuine? Or was she pleased to steer the conversation here? "Now there's an interesting character. He's been buying my designs for years, you know. Very loyal customer."

Loyal customer. Interesting word choice. Not just "customer" but "loyal." Like he owed her something.

"Is he?"

"Oh yes. Always pays cash, always buys multiple pieces at a time." She cut into her meatloaf. "He came to one of my studio sales last year. Spent hours going through everything. Very particular about what he wanted."

I took a bite of my chicken pot pie, letting her talk. People revealed more when you stayed quiet, let them fill the silence. Viola knew this too. Which meant she wanted me to know these details about Milo. But why?

"He told me he was going to be bigger than Mel Tanner someday. Very ambitious, that one." She paused, and I caught something in her expression. Pride? Satisfaction? "Though I always got the sense he was frustrated. Like he was working hard but not getting the recognition he deserved."

There. That tone. Like she understood his frustration. Like she sympathized with it.

Like maybe she'd encouraged it.

"That must be difficult."

"I imagine so." Viola sipped her coffee, watching me over the rim. "Especially when you're the one doing all the work behind the scenes while someone else takes all the credit." She looked at me meaningfully. "That can build up a lot of resentment."

Was she talking about Milo and Ethan? Or was there a message here for me? A reminder that she was watching, assessing, understanding more than I wanted her to?

I said nothing, just continued eating.

"Did they seem tense? When you saw them that morning?" Viola asked. "Milo and Ethan?"

"They were having a discussion."

"About?"

"Work, I think. Something about a fashion show."

"Interesting." Viola's expression was thoughtful. "And after? Did you see either of them again that day?"

The questions were casual, conversational. But there were too many of them. Too specific.

"I went to my shop. Worked all day." I met her eyes. "Why do you ask?"

"Just curious. You know how I am, always interested in industry gossip." She smiled, but it didn't quite reach her eyes. "I heard Milo's taking over the brand now. Moving forward with everything."

"That was fast."

"Wasn't it?" Viola took another bite. "Almost like he was prepared for it. Like he'd been planning for this opportunity."

We ate in silence for a moment. I could feel her watching me, waiting for my reaction.

"You know what else I heard?" Viola said, her tone shifting to something more confidential. "Lawrence Jung is in town. In fact, he's been meeting with Milo."

"Jung? The designer?"

"The very one. Ruthless man. Talented, but ruthless." She leaned forward. "He's been trying to poach talent from other houses for years. If he's circling Ethan's brand now..." She trailed off meaningfully.

"You think he's involved?"

"With the death?" Viola considered. "I think Jung is capable of a lot of things. But murder seems extreme, even for him." She paused. "Though there's one person I'd definitely look at if I were the police."

"Oh?"

"That model, Jamie Patton." Viola's voice dropped. "She's been causing quite a scene lately. Bad-mouthing Ethan all over town."

"Why?"

"He dropped her from his roster about six months ago. No explanation, just stopped booking her." Viola shook her head. "She's been bitter ever since. Telling anyone who'll listen that Ethan was a fraud, that he stole designs. Very vindictive."

I thought about Jamie in my shop that morning. Trying on the blue dress. Talking about leaving flowers at the memorial early, before anyone could see.

"She must have been very hurt."

"Hurt enough to do something drastic?" Viola raised an eyebrow. "That's the question, isn't it?"

Annie came by to refill our cups and clear our plates. "You ladies doing okay? Any dessert tonight?"

"Not for me," I said.

"Me neither. Just the check when you have a moment, Annie dear."

After Annie left, Viola reached across the table and took my hand. Her grip was firm, her eyes serious.

"Dora Lee, I need you to promise me something."

The shift was sudden. Too sudden. We'd gone from discussing Milo to this in seconds. What had prompted it? Had I revealed too much? Or was this planned all along?

"What's that?"

"Promise me you won't go investigating this on your own. Let the police handle it."

There it was. The real reason for all her questions. She wanted me to back off.

"I'm just an old lady, Vi. What could I possibly do?"

"That's exactly what worries me." She squeezed my hand, and I felt the strength in her fingers. Viola had always been strong. Physically and otherwise. "You're not just an old lady. You're brilliant and observant and stubborn. And if you start poking around in a murder..." She didn't finish the sentence. "I don't want anything to happen to you. You're one of my oldest friends."

Oldest friends. The phrase hung in the air between us. Not "best friends." Not "dear friends." Oldest. A statement of duration, not depth.

Forty years of this careful dance. Forty years of watching each other, measuring each other, never quite trusting but never quite cutting ties either.

"I'll be careful."

"That's not the same as promising to stay out of it." Her eyes searched mine. "Dora Lee, whoever did this, if it wasn't an accident, they're dangerous. They killed once. They could kill again."

There was something in her tone. Not quite a warning, but close.

"I understand."

She held my gaze for another moment, then released my hand and sat back. "Good. Now, tell me about the shop. How are sales?"

We shifted to easier topics. Fabric suppliers, the latest fashion trends, mutual acquaintances in the industry. Viola told me about a young designer she was mentoring, about a collection she was planning for next spring.

But even as we talked and laughed, I couldn't shake the feeling that we'd been playing a game. That Viola had been testing me, trying to figure out what I knew. And that her warnings had been less about friendship and more about something else entirely.

When Annie brought the check, Viola grabbed it before I could. "My treat tonight."

"You don't have to do that."

"I want to. Consider it a thank you for being my friend." She smiled warmly. "We've been through a lot together over the years, haven't we?"

"We have."

"And we'll get through this too. Whatever happens with this investigation, with the police sorting everything out." She stood, gathering her coat and purse. "Just remember. Some things are better left to the professionals."

We said our goodbyes on the sidewalk outside the diner. Viola kissed my cheek, then watched her climb into a ride share that was waiting for her at the curb.

I stood on the sidewalk, watching Viola's car disappear into traffic. She'd paid for dinner without asking, pressed her concerns about my safety, warned me to stay out of the investigation.

All the things a good friend would do.

So, why did I feel like I'd just been threatened?

I pulled my coat tighter and started walking home, Pippa at my side. Viola knew Milo well. Had watched him grow frustrated over the years. Had understood his resentment about being overshadowed.

Had she done more than understand? Had she fed that resentment? Encouraged it? Given him ideas about what he deserved?

I shook my head. Paranoia. I was seeing shadows everywhere.

But forty years with Viola had taught me one thing: she never did anything without a reason. And tonight, she'd wanted something from me.

She'd wanted me to stop investigating.

The question was: why?

Then Pippa and I crossed the street back to the Royal Griffen.

The memorial for Ethan had grown even larger since this morning. The sidewalk in front of the building was crowded with flowers, candles, and teddy bears. Several people stood around it, some crying, others just looking.

I recognized one of them. A young man in his early twenties with dark hair and glasses. He was placing a bouquet of white roses near the poster-sized photo.

"Excuse me, dear," I said, shuffling closer. "Did you know Ethan?"

He looked up, wiping his eyes. "Yeah. We were in design school together. Madison Institute." He gestured to the flowers. "I can't believe he's gone. He was supposed to do his first big show next week."

"I heard about that. Such a shame."

"The worst part is, Milo's canceling everything. All that work Ethan did, just... gone. Gone just like Ethan." His voice was bitter. "And now Milo's taking over the brand like Ethan never existed."

"You don't like Milo?"

"Nobody did. He was always so intense. Angry about everything." The young man straightened up. "Ethan was the nice one. The one everyone wanted to work with. Milo was just..." He trailed off, shaking his head. "Sorry. I shouldn't speak ill of people. Especially not now."

"It's alright, dear. Grief makes us all say things we might not otherwise."

"Yeah." He looked back at the memorial. "I just hope they figure out what really happened. Because I don't buy this 'accident' story. Not for a second."

"Why not?"

"Because Ethan was too smart. Too careful. He wouldn't have gotten himself locked in a sauna." He met my eyes. "Someone did this to him. I know it."

After he walked away, I stood there with Pippa, looking at the memorial. Someone had added the poster-sized photo of Ethan at a fashion show. He was smiling, confident, alive.

Next to him in the photo stood Milo, slightly in the background, slightly out of focus.

Always the sidekick, never the star.

Until now.

Walter appeared at the building entrance, coming over to check on me. "You doing alright, Miss Dora Lee? You've been standing here a while."

"Just paying my respects."

"It's a sad thing. That boy had his whole life ahead of him." Walter looked at the memorial, then back at me. "You be careful now.

There's been a lot of talk about what happened. Some folks think it wasn't an accident."

"What do you think, Walter?"

He was quiet for a moment, choosing his words carefully. "I think people don't always show us who they really are. Not until it's too late."

"That's very wise."

"My mama used to say it. She was usually right." He held the door open for me. "Come on now. Let's get you inside where it's warm."

I let him walk me to the elevator, Pippa trotting along beside us. As the elevator doors closed and I started up to my floor, I thought about everything Viola had said.

How she'd asked so many questions about what I knew.

How she'd steered the conversation toward Jamie as a suspect.

How she'd warned me, almost too insistently, to stay out of it.

And that moment when she'd said Milo was frustrated, not getting the recognition he deserved. How had she known that? Had Milo told her? Or had she known because she'd been the one encouraging that resentment?

I pushed the thought away. Viola was my friend. She'd been my friend for over forty years.

But a small seed of doubt had been planted.

And it was starting to grow.

Chapter Five

The next morning, after my treadmill session and Pippa's breakfast, I decided the shop could wait an hour or two. There was investigating to be done, and the best place to start was right here in the building.

Walter had been the doorman at the Royal Griffen for almost fifteen years. If anyone knew the comings and goings of residents, it was him. The man had a memory like a steel trap and a friendly demeanor that made people tell him things they probably shouldn't.

I found him at his usual post near the entrance, straightening his uniform jacket. When he saw me and Pippa, his face lit up with his trademark smile.

"Good morning, Miss Dora Lee! And good morning to you too, Miss Pippa!"

Pippa's tail wagged enthusiastically. She loved Walter almost as much as she loved treats.

"Good morning, Walter dear," I said, shuffling up to him slowly. "Beautiful day, isn't it?"

"Sure is. You heading out to the shop?"

"In a bit. I thought I'd sit in the lobby for a spell first. These old bones need a rest before the walk." I gestured to one of the plush chairs near his station.

"You take your time. Can I get you anything? Water? Coffee?"

"Oh, no thank you. I'm just fine." I settled into the chair with an exaggerated sigh of relief. Pippa curled up at my feet. "Such terrible business about that young man."

Walter's smile faded. "Mr. Kemper. Yes, ma'am. Terrible thing. He was always so polite, always had a kind word."

"Were you working that day? The day it happened?"

"I was. Afternoon shift." He shook his head. "I keep thinking about it. Wondering if there was something I should have noticed."

"I'm sure you did everything right, Walter. You always do." I paused, letting the compliment settle. "Did you see him that day? Ethan?"

"I did, actually. He came through the lobby around two o'clock. He and Mr. Savage had words right there." Walter pointed to a spot near the elevator. "Heated discussion, from what I could tell. Mr. Savage stormed off after that."

"Stormed off where?"

"Out the front entrance. He was wearing gym clothes, looked like he was going for a run." Walter leaned in slightly, lowering his voice even though there was no one else around. "Between you and me, Miss Dora Lee, those two had been arguing a lot lately. Past few weeks, I'd say."

"Is that so?"

"Yes, ma'am. Usually Mr. Kemper was calm, but Mr. Savage, he's got a temper on him. I've seen him snap at Miss Chelsea, at Melanie at the desk, even at some of the residents."

I thought about Milo at the diner, barking at Annie. Milo berating Ellie by the memorial. The boy certainly seemed angry at the world.

"Did you see Milo, I mean Mr. Savage, come back from his run?"

Walter thought about it. "You know, I'm not sure. My shift ended at six, and I don't recall seeing him come back through. But he could have come in through the service entrance. Some of the residents do that when they've been exercising, especially if they don't want to track through the lobby all sweaty."

"The service entrance." I repeated the words slowly. That entrance was near the gym and sauna. If Milo had come back that way, he could have accessed the gym area without Walter seeing him.

And he must have come back at some point, because when I saw him at the crime scene that evening, he'd changed out of his gym clothes. He'd been wearing one of Viola's suits. Dark, perfectly tailored. Which meant he'd been back to his apartment between the run and Ethan's death.

"Did the police ask you about this?"

"They did. That Detective Keller, she was very thorough. Asked me about everyone who came and went that day." He straightened up as someone approached the entrance from outside. "She seemed particularly interested in Mr. Savage's movements."

The door opened and Detective Keller herself walked in. She was in uniform, looking official and focused. When she saw me, something flickered across her face. Recognition, maybe a touch of annoyance.

"Miss Griffen," she said with a nod.

"Detective Keller! How lovely to see you again." I smiled sweetly. "Are you here about poor Ethan?"

"I am. Following up on some details." She glanced at Walter. "Mr. Torres, do you have a few minutes? I have some additional questions."

"Of course, Detective." Walter looked apologetic as he turned to me. "Miss Dora Lee, if you'll excuse me."

"Oh, certainly, certainly." I started to stand, making a show of it being difficult.

"Actually, Miss Griffen," Detective Keller said. "Since you're here, I'd like to ask you a few questions as well. Would you mind waiting?"

"Not at all, dear. I have all the time in the world."

Detective Keller pulled Walter a few steps away, speaking to him in low tones. I couldn't hear everything, but I caught snippets. Something about the security cameras in the lobby, about timing, about who had access to the gym area.

I sat back down, pretending to be absorbed in watching Pippa. She'd gotten up and was now sitting pretty, her front paws raised in her begging position, staring at Walter's jacket pocket where he usually kept treats.

"Not now, Miss Pippa," Walter said with a quiet chuckle, patting his pocket. "After I'm done talking to the Detective."

Pippa's ears drooped slightly, but she maintained her position, ever the optimist.

Detective Keller and Walter moved even further away, and their voices dropped to whispers. I couldn't make out the words anymore.

After about five minutes, Detective Keller finished with Walter and came over to me. She pulled up a chair, sitting down with her notepad in hand.

"Miss Griffen, I have a few follow-up questions if you don't mind."

"Of course, dear. Happy to help."

"You mentioned the other night that you rode the elevator with Mr. Kemper the morning he died. Can you walk me through that encounter again? Any additional details you might have remembered?"

"Well, let me see. Pippa and I were heading to the shop. The elevator opened and there were Ethan and Milo already inside, having quite the discussion."

"About what?"

"Oh, they were having quite the discussion about work. Something about a fashion show and models and deadlines. Ethan seemed calm, but Milo seemed frustrated." I waved my hand dismissively. "But what do I know? I'm just an old lady. I probably misunderstood."

"You seem to have understood quite a bit, Miss Griffen." There was something sharp in her tone now. "For someone who's hard of hearing."

My stomach tightened. I might have overplayed my hand.

"Oh, they were shouting, dear. Practically yelling. Hard not to hear that." I smiled innocently.

Detective Keller studied me for a long moment. I could see the calculation in her eyes, the reassessment. This one was smarter than I'd given her credit for.

"Miss Griffen, if you remember anything else, anything at all, please contact me." She handed me a business card. "Even small details can be important."

"Of course, Detective. Always happy to help."

She stood, tucking her notepad away. "One more thing. Where were you between two and five pm on the day Mr. Kemper died?"

So, it was murder. They had a time of death window. My pulse picked up speed, but I kept my breathing steady and my expression mild.

"At my shop, dear. I'm always at my shop during the day. Open from nine to five, Tuesday through Saturday."

"Can anyone verify that?"

"Well, I had a customer come in that morning. She bought two dresses. And I was working on alterations all afternoon. Pippa was with me the whole time." I gestured to my dog, who had finally given up on Walter and returned to my feet.

"I see. Thank you for your time, Miss Griffen."

She walked away toward the elevator, probably heading up to question more residents. I stayed in my chair, sorting through what had just happened.

Two to five pm. That's when it happened. Milo had stormed out around two, according to Walter. I'd seen him running past my shop window sometime in the afternoon, though I couldn't remember exactly when.

And now Detective Keller was clearly suspicious of me paying too much attention.

"Fiddlesticks," I muttered under my breath.

Walter came back over once the Detective was gone, pulling a small dog biscuit from his pocket. "Alright, Miss Pippa. You earned this for your patience."

Pippa took it delicately, her tail wagging, then settled back at my feet to enjoy her prize.

"Everything okay, Miss Dora Lee?" Walter asked.

"Oh yes, just fine. Just fine." I stood up, this time moving with a bit more of my actual agility before catching myself and slowing down. "I should get to the shop. Come along, Pippa."

"You have a good day now. And Miss Dora Lee?" Walter's voice stopped me at the door. "You be careful, you hear? I don't like the way that Detective was looking at you. Like she thinks you know more than you're saying."

"I'm always careful, Walter."

"I hope so."

As Pippa and I walked out into the morning sunshine, I thought about what he'd said. Detective Keller was no fool, and if I kept poking around too obviously, she might start looking at me as more than just a harmless old busybody.

But I couldn't stop now. Not when things were getting interesting.

The walk to the shop gave me time to think. Detective Keller's question about my whereabouts had been pointed. They were treating this as a homicide investigation, no doubt about it. The sauna accident was no accident at all.

I unlocked the shop and went through my usual routine, getting Pippa settled in her window bed and turning on all the lights. The blue silk dress that Jamie had looked at yesterday was still on the rack, exactly where she'd left it.

I pulled it out and hung it on one of the display hooks near the dressing rooms. The silk caught the morning light, the blue seeming to shift and shimmer. It really was a beautiful piece, one I'd finished just last month. The cut was classic with just enough modern flair to make it interesting.

I was rearranging a display of scarves when my phone buzzed in my pocket. A text from Viola.

"Morning! How are you feeling today? You seemed a bit distracted at dinner last night."

I stared at the message. Distracted? I'd thought I'd hidden it well.

I typed back: "Just tired. Long week."

Her response came immediately: "I hope you're not still thinking about that Kemper situation. Remember what I said about letting the professionals handle it."

There it was again. That insistence that I stay out of it.

"Of course. Just going about my business."

"Good. Let's have lunch soon. I miss our chats."

"That would be lovely."

I put my phone away, but the exchange left me unsettled. Why was Viola so interested in whether I was investigating? And how had she known I seemed distracted? I'd been careful at dinner, or so I'd thought.

The bell over the door chimed, pulling me from my thoughts.

Jamie Patton stood in the doorway, looking slightly uncertain.

"Oh, hello again, dear," I said with a warm smile.

"Hi, Miss Dora Lee. I, um, I hope you don't mind me coming back. I couldn't stop thinking about that blue silk dress from yesterday."

"The one you were looking at? I pulled it out this morning, actually. It's right over here." I gestured to where I'd hung it.

Her face lit up. "Really? Mind if I try it on again? I know I was wearing it just yesterday, but I want to make sure before I commit."

"Of course, dear. Take your time."

She took the dress and disappeared into the dressing room. I heard the rustle of fabric as she changed.

A few minutes later, she emerged.

"It really does look stunning on you," I said. "Even better than yesterday, somehow."

She turned to look at herself in the full-length mirror again, smoothing the fabric over her hips. "I love it. I really do love it." Then her face fell slightly. "Though I'm still not sure where I'd wear it. I don't get booked for the fancy events much anymore."

"Well, you never know when an opportunity might come up. It's always good to have something beautiful hanging in your closet, just in case."

She laughed, but it carried that same bitter edge from yesterday. "You're right. Maybe I should just buy nice things for myself instead of waiting for some designer to hire me so I can wear their clothes."

I moved to the seating area near the dressing rooms, lowering myself carefully into one of the vintage chairs I kept there for customers. "Sit with me for a moment, dear. If you have time."

She hesitated, then sat down in the chair across from me, still wearing the dress. Pippa wandered over from her window perch and sniffed at Jamie's shoes.

"You mentioned yesterday that Ethan stopped booking you," I said gently. "That must have been hard on your career."

"It was. It is." She reached down to pet Pippa absently. "I mean, I'm still working. I'm not broke or anything. But Ethan was on his way up, you know? Being associated with him, being one of his girls, that would have opened doors. Instead, he just cut me loose with no explanation."

"Did you ever find out why?"

"No. And I tried. I called, I emailed, I even showed up at his studio once." She winced at the memory. "That was humiliating. He wouldn't even see me. Milo came out and told me Ethan was going in a different direction with his models. Like I was a piece of furniture he was redecorating around."

"That's awful, dear."

"The worst part is, I don't even know what I did wrong. Did I gain weight? Did I say something stupid at a shoot? Did someone else spread rumors about me?" She threw up her hands. "In this industry, you can be blacklisted and never even know why."

"It sounds like you were quite angry with him."

"I was. I am. I mean, I was." She caught herself, shaking her head. "God, that sounds terrible, doesn't it? The guy's dead and I'm still bitter about not getting booked."

"You're allowed to have complicated feelings, honey. Just because someone died doesn't mean they were perfect or that they didn't hurt people when they were alive."

Jamie looked at me with something like relief. "Thank you for saying that. Everyone's acting like Ethan was this amazing, generous soul, and I'm over here thinking about the same Ethan who ghosted half his models and stole design ideas from his interns."

My attention sharpened. "He stole designs?"

"Oh yeah. Everyone knew it. He'd have these young kids working for him, desperate for experience and a credit on their resume, and he'd just take their sketches and claim them as his own." She leaned forward. "There was this one girl who worked for him last summer. She created this whole collection based on Japanese street fashion, super innovative stuff. Two months later, Ethan's showing pieces that look exactly like her work, and she's not mentioned anywhere."

"Did she confront him?"

"She tried. He threatened to blacklist her from the industry if she made a fuss. Said he'd tell everyone she was difficult to work with, that she'd stolen from him." Jamie shook her head. "She ended up dropping out of fashion entirely. Last I heard, she's working at a bookstore in Portland."

So, Ethan wasn't quite the rising star everyone wanted to believe he was. He had enemies, people with legitimate grievances.

"What about Milo? Was he aware of all this?"

"Milo?" Jamie snorted. "Milo enabled it. He handled all the business side, all the contracts. He made sure those interns signed NDAs so they couldn't talk about what went on in the studio. He was just as bad as Ethan, maybe worse because he was the one protecting him."

"But they argued a lot, didn't they? I heard they'd been fighting recently."

Jamie nodded. "Yeah, things got tense the last few months. I think Milo was tired of being in Ethan's shadow. He's actually really talented in his own right, but nobody paid attention to him because Ethan was the front man, the face of the brand." She stood up, walking back to the mirror. "Honestly, I wouldn't be surprised if Milo's relieved Ethan's gone. Now he gets to be the star."

"That's quite an accusation."

"Is it though?" She met my eyes in the mirror. "Ethan dies under mysterious circumstances, and within twenty-four hours, Milo's taking over the brand and making plans. Seems pretty convenient to me."

She went back into the dressing room to change. I sat there piecing together what she'd told me. Ethan as a design thief. Milo as his enabler and protector. Both of them apparently ruthless when it came to their careers.

Jamie emerged a few minutes later, the blue dress draped carefully over her arm. "I'll take it. I don't care if I never have anywhere to wear it. It's too beautiful to leave behind."

"Wonderful. I think it was meant for you."

As I rang her up, she hesitated, her card hovering over the reader. "Miss Dora Lee, can I ask you something?"

"Of course, dear."

"Do you think someone killed him? Ethan, I mean. Everyone's saying it was an accident, but..." She trailed off.

"What do you think?"

"I think Ethan made a lot of people angry. I think he burned a lot of bridges. And I think that sauna door didn't just malfunction on its own." She tapped her card and the transaction went through. "But that's just my opinion."

"Well, I'm sure the police will figure it out."

"Yeah." She took the bag with her dress. "Thanks for this. And thanks for listening. You're easy to talk to."

"Anytime, honey. You come back anytime."

After she left, I stood at the window, watching her walk down the street. Pippa came over and sat at my feet, leaning against my leg.

"Well, Pippa, we learned quite a bit this morning, didn't we?"

She tilted her head, those oversized ears flopping.

"Ethan was a thief and possibly a bully. Milo was his accomplice. And Jamie Patton had every reason to want Ethan out of the picture." I bent down to scratch behind Pippa's ears. "But does that make her a killer? Or is she just another person he wronged?"

The rest of the afternoon was quiet. I worked on some alterations, hemming a pair of pants for Mrs. Chen from the third floor and taking in a jacket for one of my regulars. My hands moved automatically, stitching and pinning, while my thoughts kept returning to the case.

Milo with motive and opportunity. Jamie with anger and hurt. Lawrence Jung circling like a vulture. And Viola, asking too many questions and steering me toward certain suspects.

By the time I locked up at five, I had more questions than answers. But I was starting to see a picture of who Ethan Kemper really was, and it wasn't the golden boy everyone wanted to remember.

Chapter Six

Back at the penthouse, I changed into comfortable loungewear: soft gray sweatpants and an oversized sweater with a geometric pattern in shades of purple and teal. My feet were happy to be out of shoes and into my fuzzy slippers.

Pippa had already claimed her spot on the couch, curled into a tight ball.

I couldn't settle though. I paced from the living room to the kitchen and back again. The questions kept circling. The pieces kept shifting. Every time I thought I had it figured out, something else didn't fit.

"Okay, Dora Lee," I said to myself. "Time to organize this properly."

I retrieved a yellow legal pad and one of my favorite pens from my desk and settled into my reading chair by the window. From here, I could see the city lights beginning to twinkle as dusk settled over the city.

At the top of the page, I wrote: **ETHAN KEMPER - MURDER**

Because that's what it was. No matter what the official story said, someone had killed that boy.

I stared at the blank page beneath the heading. Where to start?

With the suspects, obviously. I wrote the word, then paused. Three names came to mind immediately.

SUSPECTS:

Milo Savage. I pressed the pen to paper and started listing what I knew. *Business partner and roommate. Argued with Ethan constantly. Walter said they'd had a heated fight around two, right before Milo stormed out in gym clothes.*

I tapped the pen against my chin. The service entrance. If Milo came back that way, no one at the front desk would have seen him. He could have accessed the gym without being noticed.

And he'd been wearing different clothes at the crime scene. One of Viola's suits. Which meant he'd come back to the apartment to change.

I kept writing. *Stands to inherit Ethan's brand. Gets to be the star instead of the sidekick. Has a temper.*

I'd seen that myself. Angry at everyone.

Viola's words from dinner came back to me. He told me once he was going to be bigger than Mel Tanner. Very ambitious. But she'd also said he was frustrated, overshadowed. That could build a lot of resentment.

And then there was his performance at the crime scene. All those tears that dried up so quickly. Already making plans to take over the brand within twenty-four hours.

I moved on to the next name.

Jamie Patton. Model dropped by Ethan six months ago with no explanation. Her career had suffered from losing that association. She'd been bitter about it, that much was clear from both our conversations.

She'd called Ethan a thief and a bully. Said he stole from interns. But she'd also left flowers at his memorial early in the morning, before anyone could see. What did that mean?

I thought about the way she'd talked about him. The anger mixed with hurt. And she'd come to my shop twice. Like she needed to talk about it. To process it with someone.

The third name felt less certain, but I wrote it anyway.

Lawrence Jung. Rival designer. Always second place to Ethan in school, with mentors, landing internships. Now he was in town, meeting with Milo, circling the brand.

Viola had called him ruthless. Said he poached talent from other designers. But murder? That seemed extreme even for someone ambitious.

I started a new section.

VICTIM - WHO WAS ETHAN REALLY?

This was important. Understanding who Ethan was might help me understand who killed him.

Rising star, everyone said. Mentored by Mel Tanner. Sweet demeanor, at least on the surface. I'd seen that myself in the elevator. The way he'd walked me to my shop, so polite and kind.

But there was another Ethan. The one who stole designs from desperate interns. Who threatened to blacklist people who confronted him. Who dropped models without explanation. Who'd driven at least one young designer out of fashion entirely.

The golden boy wasn't so golden after all.

I turned to a new page and wrote: **TIMELINE - DAY OF MURDER**

This was where the details mattered. I started at the beginning.

Morning - I'd seen Ethan and Milo in the elevator. They were arguing about the fashion show, about models and deadlines. Ethan wanted to push the show back. Milo was frustrated, angry.

Around 2pm - Walter said they'd argued again in the lobby. Milo stormed out in gym clothes, heading for a run.

Time of death - Detective Keller's questions had made it clear. Between two and five pm. A three-hour window.

I'd seen Milo running past my shop window. When exactly? I closed my eyes, trying to remember. Mid-afternoon. Maybe three? I couldn't be sure.

Then Ethan was found dead in the sauna. The door had malfunctioned, they said. But there was an emergency latch inside. It should have worked.

The rescue team had to pry the door open. I'd seen the splintered wood, the twisted metal frame. And those scratch marks near where the inside handle would have been.

Someone had jammed that door from the outside. Someone had trapped him in there deliberately.

I started a new section: **QUESTIONS**

My pen hovered over the paper. What didn't I know? What did I need to find out?

How exactly was the sauna door jammed? I needed to see that door again, examine it more closely. But it was probably evidence now, taken away by the police.

Who had access to the gym area? Residents, obviously. But the service entrance required a keycard. Did Milo have one? Did he need one if he lived in the building?

Where was Milo between 2 and 5pm? He said he went for a run. No witnesses. Convenient.

Did anyone see Ethan go to the gym? Someone must have. He didn't just materialize in that sauna.

Why the sauna specifically? Why not somewhere else? Was it planned or opportunistic?

Who else might have wanted Ethan dead? I'd found three suspects. Were there others I didn't know about?

I sat back, studying my notes spread across two pages. The evidence pointed to Milo. The motive was there. The opportunity was there. The suspicious behavior was there.

But something nagged at me. It felt too neat. Too obvious.

Then again, sometimes the obvious answer was the right answer.

A knock at the door made me jump. My pen skittered across the page, leaving a dark line through my notes. Pippa's head popped up, and she let out a small warning bark.

"Shush, Pippa. I'm sure it's just someone from the building."

But my pulse had picked up. It was after nine at night. Who would be knocking at this hour?

I shuffled to the door, forcing myself back into the harmless old lady role. I looked through the peephole.

Milo Savage stood in the hallway, swaying slightly.

My chest tightened. I'd been sitting here writing about him, analyzing whether he was a murderer, and now he was at my door.

I cracked the door open, keeping the chain on.

"Yes?"

"Miss Dora Lee?" His words were slightly slurred. He'd been drinking. "I need to talk to someone."

"It's quite late, dear."

"Please. I just... I need to talk." He ran a hand through his hair, and I could see his eyes were red-rimmed. Not just from alcohol, I realized. These were eyes that hadn't seen proper sleep in days. "You're the only one who doesn't look at me like I'm a monster."

Every instinct told me to send him away. To keep that chain on and tell him to come back tomorrow when he was sober.

But he might say something useful. Something incriminating. Or something that proved his innocence.

I closed the door, unlatched the chain, and opened it again. My hand stayed near the doorframe, ready to slam it shut if needed.

"Come in, but just for a moment. I was about to go to bed."

He stumbled in, and I caught a strong whiff of whiskey. Pippa's growl was low and continuous, a sound I'd rarely heard from her. She stayed on the couch, but her body was tense, alert.

"Sit down before you fall down," I said, gesturing to the armchair across from the couch.

He collapsed into it, his head falling into his hands. His shoulders shook, and for a moment I thought he was crying. But when he looked up, his eyes were dry. Just haunted.

"Everyone thinks I did it. I can see it in their eyes. The police, the neighbors, everyone at the building."

"Did what, dear?" I lowered myself onto the couch slowly, keeping Pippa between us. My legal pad sat on the side table, face down now. I didn't want him to see what I'd been writing.

"Killed Ethan!" He looked up at me. Genuine anguish twisted his features. Or was he just a good actor? "They think I killed my best friend for his stupid brand."

"Did you?"

He blinked at me. The bluntness of my question seemed to cut through the alcohol fog. Then he let out a bitter laugh that sounded more like a sob.

"No. God, no. I loved that guy. He was like my brother." He leaned back, staring at the ceiling. His hands gripped the armrests, knuckles white. "Sure, we fought. We fought all the time. He was a dreamer and I was the realist, and we butted heads constantly. But I would never..."

He trailed off, and I noticed his hands had started shaking. He pulled them into his lap, pressing them together as if trying to stop the tremor.

"Then why are you here, telling me this?"

"Because everyone else has already decided I'm guilty!" His voice rose. Pippa stood up on the couch, her growl deepening. He seemed to notice and lowered his voice. "Sorry. Sorry. I just... you're the only one who doesn't look at me like that."

"I'm just an old lady, dear. What do I know about anything?"

He studied me for a long moment. There was an intelligence in his eyes that the alcohol hadn't completely dulled. I kept my breathing steady, my expression mildly confused.

"You remind me of my grandmother," he said finally. "She died two years ago. She was sharp as anything, even at ninety. Everyone thought she was just this sweet old lady, but she saw everything. Knew everything." A sad smile crossed his face. "She would have liked you."

I didn't know what to say to that, so I stayed quiet.

"Ethan was my best friend, but he was also the most frustrating person I've ever known." The words started spilling out now like he'd been holding them in too long. His voice had that quality of someone who needed to confess something, anything, just to stop the thoughts in his head. "He had all this talent, all this charisma, and he just threw it around like it didn't matter. Meanwhile, I'm doing all the actual work, managing the business, making sure we don't go bankrupt, and nobody even knows my name."

"That must have been difficult."

"You have no idea. Do you know what it's like to pour your heart into something and watch someone else take all the credit?" He leaned forward, elbows on his knees, and I noticed his hands were still shaking. He clasped them together tighter. "I designed half the pieces in that collection. Half! But it's Ethan's brand, Ethan's vision, Ethan's big debut."

"So, you were angry with him."

"Of course I was angry with him! But I didn't kill him!" He stood up abruptly, then swayed. Pippa barked, sharp and warning. I tensed, ready to move if I needed to.

But he just paced to the window, putting distance between us. He pressed his forehead against the glass, his breath fogging it. "Everyone keeps asking me where I was, what I was doing. I went for a run. That's it. Just a run to clear my head after our fight. When I got back, he was..." His voice cracked. His hand came up to the window frame, gripping it so hard I could see the tendons stand out. "He was already dead."

The way he said it made something tighten in my chest. There was too much emotion there. Too much specificity. Like he was seeing it again, right now, in front of him.

"What time did you get back?"

He turned to look at me. Suspicion flickered across his face. "Why do you want to know?"

My mouth went dry. I'd pushed too hard. Asked too directly.

"Just curious, dear. I'm a nosy old lady. It's what we do."

The suspicion faded, replaced by exhaustion. "Around four-thirty, I think. Maybe a little later. I ran all the way to Central Park and back. Needed to burn off the anger." He rubbed his face with both hands. "I don't know. Time gets weird when you're that upset. Everything blurs together."

"Did anyone see you?"

"I don't know. Maybe? I wasn't exactly paying attention." He moved away from the window, heading toward the door. His gait was unsteady, whether from alcohol or something else, I couldn't tell. "I should go. I don't even know why I came up here. I've had too much to drink and I'm not making sense."

"Why are you telling me all this, dear?" I asked, keeping my voice gentle and confused.

He paused at the door, his hand on the knob. When he looked back at me, there was something desperate in his eyes. Something that looked almost like a plea.

"Because you remind me of my grandmother," he said again. "And because I think you actually listen instead of just waiting to accuse me." He pulled the door open. "Thank you for not calling security on the drunk guy ranting at you."

"Get some rest, dear. Things will look better in the morning."

"Yeah. Maybe." He stepped into the hallway, then turned back one more time. "Miss Dora Lee? If you hear anything, if anyone says anything about that day... will you let me know?"

"Of course, dear."

He nodded and shuffled away toward the elevator. I watched until he was inside and the doors closed, then I shut and locked my door. The chain went back on. Then I pushed one of my dining chairs under the doorknob for extra measure.

My hands trembled as I released the chair back. My heart was pounding. I'd just been alone with a potential murderer.

Pippa jumped down from the couch and pressed against my legs, whining softly.

"It's okay, girl. I'm okay." I bent down to pet her. She licked my hand, then my face, checking me over.

I went back to my chair and picked up my legal pad, flipping to a new page. I needed to write this down while it was fresh.

MILO'S VISIT:

Drunk, emotional. Smelled like whiskey. Came to my door after 9pm.

Claims he loved Ethan like a brother. But admits to being angry about getting no credit for his work. Says he designed half the collection.

Physical observations: hands shaking (tried to hide it), eyes red-rimmed (days of no sleep?), gripped window frame so hard tendons stood out, swayed when he stood (alcohol or emotional state?).

Went for run to Central Park after the 2pm fight with Ethan. Claims he returned around 4:30pm. Maybe later, he said. Not sure. Says no one saw him. Said "time gets weird when you're that upset."

When he said "when I got back, he was already dead" - the way he gripped that window frame, the way his voice broke. Too much detail? Or genuine grief?

Genuinely upset or good actor? Hard to tell. The pain in his voice when he talked about Ethan seemed real. But killers can be good liars. Or maybe killers who didn't mean to kill feel genuine pain too.

Wanted to know if I hear anything. Fishing for information? Or innocent man desperate to prove himself?

Compared me to his grandmother. He said she saw everything, knew everything. Does he suspect I'm not as harmless as I seem?

Note: *He said he "needed to tell someone" - tell someone what? Just that he's innocent? Or something more?*

I set the pad down and stared out at the city lights. Milo's visit had complicated everything. He seemed genuinely distraught, but that could be guilt as easily as grief. And his timeline put him right in the window when Ethan died.

But something about it all still didn't sit right. The way he talked about Ethan. The pain in his voice when he said his friend was dead. Either he was an exceptional liar, or there was more to this story than a simple case of ambition-driven murder.

"What do you think, Pippa?"

She tilted her head, ears flopping.

"Yeah, I don't know either."

I got ready for bed, but I knew sleep would be elusive tonight. I kept playing the conversation over in my mind. Looking for the lie. Looking for the truth.

One thing was certain: I needed to find out exactly where Milo had been between two and five pm. And I needed to figure out how that sauna door had been jammed from the outside.

Because whoever killed Ethan Kemper had planned it carefully. And they were still out there, watching everyone scramble to make sense of it all.

Chapter Seven

I woke up the next morning with a stiff neck from tossing and turning all night. My dreams had been full of locked doors and scratching sounds and Milo's desperate face asking me over and over, "Why doesn't anyone believe me?"

I sat up in bed and rubbed my neck. "Enough of that. Today is a work day. Focus on work."

After my treadmill routine and Pippa's breakfast, I chose my outfit carefully. A vintage Diane von Furstenberg-inspired wrap dress in a bold orange and pink floral print, paired with cream-colored tights and my comfortable burgundy ankle boots. A long beaded necklace in complementary colors and my favorite chunky bracelet completed the look.

"What do you think, Pip?"

She wagged her tail, which I took as approval.

The morning at the shop started quietly. I spent the first hour working on Mrs. Noble's alteration, a simple hem on a pair of vintage trousers she'd found at an estate sale. The fabric was lovely, a soft wool blend that had held up beautifully over the years.

My phone buzzed. A text from Viola.

"Thinking of you. Coffee soon? Need to catch up properly. xo"

I stared at the message for a moment. Something about the timing felt odd, coming right after Milo's late-night visit. But maybe I was being paranoid.

"Sounds lovely. Let me know when," I texted back.

Around ten-thirty, the bell chimed and a woman I didn't recognize walked in. She was probably in her mid-forties, well-dressed in that careful way that spoke of someone who paid attention to quality.

"Good morning," I said warmly. "Welcome to Dora Lee's."

"Good morning. I'm looking for something specific, if you do custom work?"

"I certainly do. What did you have in mind?"

She pulled out her phone, showing me a photo of a dress. "I saw something like this in a magazine, but I can't find it anywhere in my size. I'm wondering if you could make something similar? Not a copy, exactly, but inspired by it?"

I studied the image. It was a cocktail dress with a fitted bodice and a full skirt, done in a deep emerald green. The neckline was interesting, an asymmetrical cut that would be flattering on the right figure.

"I can absolutely do something like this. When do you need it by?"

"I have an event in six weeks. Is that enough time?"

"More than enough. Let me take your measurements and we can talk about fabric choices."

For the next forty-five minutes, we discussed colors, fabrics, the exact style she wanted. She was easy to work with, trusting my expertise but clear about her preferences. By the time she left, having put down a deposit, I was energized in a way I hadn't felt in months.

After she left, I looked at my fabric supplies and realized I didn't have quite what I needed for her dress. I wanted something with more weight than what I had on hand, something that would hold the full skirt properly.

"Pippa, I think we need to take a field trip."

She looked up from her window bed, interested.

I pulled out my phone and requested a ride to the fabric district. Ten minutes later, Pippa and I were settling into the back of a sedan, heading downtown.

The driver, a chatty man named Luis, tried to make conversation.

"Beautiful day, yes?"

"Yes, lovely," I said.

"You going shopping?"

"Fabric shopping. I'm a designer."

"Ah! Fashion!" He gestured enthusiastically, nearly swerving into another lane. "My daughter, she loves fashion. Always watching the shows on TV, making sketches."

"How old is she?"

"Fifteen. She says she wants to go to design school. I tell her, 'Mija, you need to be practical. Get a business degree.' But she doesn't listen." He laughed. "Young people, they have dreams."

"Dreams are important," I said. "The world needs more people who create beautiful things."

He nodded thoughtfully. "Maybe you are right. Maybe I worry too much."

When we arrived at the fabric district, I thanked him and gave him a generous tip. "Tell your daughter to keep designing. The world has enough business majors."

His smile was brilliant. "I will tell her. Thank you, señora."

The fabric district was one of my favorite places in the city. Blocks and blocks of shops, each crammed with bolts of fabric in every color and texture imaginable. The air smelled of sizing and dye, and even on a Thursday morning, it was bustling with designers, costumers, and crafters.

Pippa trotted along beside me happily. She'd been coming here with me since she was a puppy, and the shop owners all knew her.

I headed straight to Goldstein's, my preferred supplier for high-quality materials. The shop had been in the same family for three generations, and old Mr. Goldstein himself was usually behind the counter.

Today was no exception.

"Dora Lee!" He called out when I walked in, his thick Brooklyn accent as comforting as an old sweater. "And Miss Pippa! Come, come. What brings you in today?"

"I need something special, Morris. A cocktail dress, emerald green or something close to it. Needs good weight for a full skirt."

"Emerald green, full skirt." He was already moving through the shop, his hands running over bolts of fabric with the expertise of fifty years in the business. "I have just the thing. Came in last week."

He pulled out a bolt of fabric that made me catch my breath. It was a silk-wool blend in a deep, rich green that seemed to shimmer when the light hit it.

"Oh, Morris."

"I know, I know. Beautiful, yes?" He draped some over his arm. "Feel the weight. Perfect for what you need."

He was right. The fabric had exactly the structure I needed while still having movement and life to it.

"How much do I need?"

"For a full skirt? Four, maybe five yards to be safe. You want matching thread, yes?"

"Yes, and I'll need some interfacing for the bodice."

We spent the next twenty minutes gathering everything I needed. Morris threw in a remnant of beautiful lace "just because" and refused to let me pay for it.

"You've been coming here for how long? Forty years?"

"Closer to fifty, Morris."

"Fifty years! So, I give you some lace. It's nothing."

I kissed his weathered cheek. "You're a mensch, Morris Goldstein."

"Yeah, yeah. Go make something beautiful."

With my supplies carefully wrapped and tucked into my large tote bag, Pippa and I walked a few blocks to catch another ride. But as we passed a small park, I noticed a familiar figure sitting on a bench.

Ellie Lands, Milo's girlfriend, was crying quietly, a tissue pressed to her face.

I hesitated. I should probably just keep walking. But something about the slump of her shoulders, the way she seemed so alone, pulled at me.

"Come on, Pippa."

I shuffled over to the bench, moving slowly and carefully.

"Excuse me, dear? Are you alright?"

Ellie looked up, and I could see her eyes were swollen from crying. When she recognized me, she tried to pull herself together.

"Oh, Miss Dora Lee. I'm fine. Just having a moment."

"May I sit?"

"Of course."

I lowered myself onto the bench, and Pippa immediately put her front paws on Ellie's knee, looking up at her with those big eyes.

"Oh, hi sweetheart." Ellie scratched behind Pippa's ears, and a small smile broke through the tears. "She's so sweet."

"She has good instincts about people. She knows when someone needs a friend."

Ellie laughed wetly. "I could use one of those right now."

We sat in silence for a moment. I'd learned that sometimes people just needed space to gather their thoughts before they could talk.

"Milo and I had a fight," she finally said. "A big one. He's been drinking so much since Ethan died, and he's paranoid that everyone thinks he's a murderer. He keeps asking me if I think he did it."

"What do you tell him?"

"I tell him of course not. I tell him I know he loved Ethan. But honestly?" She looked at me, her eyes desperate. "I don't know anymore. I don't know anything anymore. He's been so angry, and he lies about stupid things, and I just don't know who I'm dating."

"That sounds very difficult."

"The worst part is, I feel guilty for even questioning him. What kind of girlfriend suspects her boyfriend of murder?" She wiped at her tears. "But then I remember that fight they had the morning Ethan died, and how angry Milo was, and I think what if?"

"What fight?"

"They were screaming at each other in the apartment. I wasn't there, but Milo told me about it later. Ethan wanted to bring in another business partner, someone with more fashion industry connections. Milo felt like he was being pushed out of his own company." She shook her head. "He was furious."

This was new information. So, there was more to their fight than just the fashion show timeline.

"Did he tell the police about this?"

"I don't know. I don't think so. He told me he just said they had a disagreement about the show." She looked at me anxiously. "Should I tell them? Is that betraying him?"

"I think you need to tell the truth, dear. If Milo is innocent, then the truth will help prove that. If he's not..." I trailed off meaningfully.

"If he's not, then I've been sleeping next to a murderer." She shuddered. "I think I need to stay somewhere else for a while. Just until this all gets sorted out."

"That sounds like a wise idea."

We sat for a few more minutes, watching people walk by, watching Pippa sniff at interesting spots on the ground. Finally, Ellie stood up.

"Thank you for sitting with me. And for not thinking I'm terrible for doubting him."

"You're not terrible. You're being careful. There's a difference."

She gave me a watery smile and walked away, pulling out her phone as she went.

I sat there a bit longer, thinking. So, Ethan had wanted to bring in a new business partner. That would have diminished Milo's role even further, maybe even pushed him out entirely. That was a much stronger motive than just professional jealousy.

"Come on, Pippa. Let's get some lunch."

The diner was moderately busy when we arrived. Martin was at his usual spot at the counter, and he nodded to me as I came in.

Annie waved from across the room. "Be right with you, hon!"

I slid into our regular booth, and Pippa hopped up beside me, settling in for her inevitable treat.

"Busy day?" Annie asked when she came over with coffee.

"Productive. Went to the fabric district."

"Find anything good?"

"The most beautiful emerald green silk-wool blend you've ever seen. I'm making a cocktail dress."

"Fancy. The usual for lunch?"

"Please."

As Annie walked away, Martin turned on his stool to look at me.

"You doing okay, Dora Lee?"

I was surprised. Martin wasn't usually one for conversation beyond a grunt or a nod.

"I'm fine, Martin. Why do you ask?"

"You've seemed distracted lately. Ever since that boy died in your building." He took a sip of his coffee. "Just want to make sure you're alright."

"That's kind of you. I'm alright. Just thinking about things."

He nodded, seeming to understand. "My wife used to say I thought too much. 'Martin,' she'd say, 'sometimes a thing is just a thing. You don't need to turn it over and over like a rock tumbler.'" He smiled at the memory. "She was usually right."

"She sounds like a wise woman."

"She was." He turned back to his food, and I knew the conversation was over. But it had been nice, that moment of connection.

Annie brought my lunch, and I ate slowly, savoring the simple pleasure of a well-made sandwich and crispy fries. Pippa got her scrambled eggs and bacon, which she demolished in record time.

By the time we made it back to the shop, it was past one o'clock. I spent the rest of the afternoon working on various projects, but my mind kept drifting back to what Ellie had told me.

Ethan had wanted a new business partner. Milo would have been pushed aside. That changed everything.

As I locked up at five, I made a mental note to add this to my legal pad when I got home. The picture was getting clearer, but I still couldn't see all of it.

Not yet.

But I would. I was certain of that.

Chapter Eight

The next morning, I was working at my sewing table when there was a knock at the door. I glanced at the clock. Nine-thirty on the dot.

"That'll be Georgie, Pippa."

Pippa's tail wagged. She loved Georgie, probably because Georgie always snuck her treats despite my protests.

I opened the door to find Georgie Mercer with her cleaning cart, her kind face breaking into a smile when she saw me.

"Morning, Miss Dora Lee. Friday cleaning day."

"Come in, come in. You want some coffee before you start?"

"Oh, I shouldn't. I've got three more apartments after yours."

"Nonsense. Sit for five minutes. When's the last time you sat down?"

She laughed, a warm sound that filled my small kitchen as she followed me in. "You might have a point there."

I poured us both coffee and we settled at my little breakfast table. Pippa immediately went to Georgie, putting her head on Georgie's knee.

"There's my girl," Georgie said, scratching behind Pippa's ears. "How've you been, sweet pea?"

"She's been spoiled as always," I said. "How are your boys?"

Georgie rolled her eyes but smiled. "Tommy finally got that job at the warehouse, thank the Lord. Marcus is still living in my basement playing video games. Says he's 'between opportunities.'"

"And the younger two?"

"David's doing good in school, but Jesse..." She shook her head. "That boy is going to give me gray hair. Sixteen years old and thinks he knows everything."

"They all do at that age."

"My mama's been asking about you, by the way. Wants to know when you're coming to visit again."

"How is she doing?"

"Good days and bad days. Yesterday was a good day. She made me teach her how to use the tablet my brother got her." Georgie chuckled. "Today she'll probably forget she even has it."

We sipped our coffee in comfortable silence. I'd known Georgie for almost ten years now, since she started working at the building. She was one of the few people I genuinely liked.

"Georgie, can I ask you something?"

"Course."

"You clean Ethan and Milo's apartment, don't you? The one on the fifth floor?"

"I do. Been cleaning for them for about two years now."

"What were they like? As residents, I mean."

She considered this, wrapping both hands around her coffee mug. "Ethan was sweet. Always thanked me, asked about my family. Left nice tips around the holidays." She paused. "Milo was different."

"Different how?"

"Not mean, exactly. Just intense. Always on his phone, always stressed about something. He'd barely notice I was there most days." She looked at me carefully. "Why are you asking?"

"Just curious. It's such a terrible thing, what happened."

"It is." She took another sip of coffee. "I'll tell you something though, and you didn't hear it from me."

I leaned forward slightly.

"The week before Ethan died, I was cleaning their apartment. They didn't know I was there yet, I'd let myself in like always. They were in the bedroom, and I could hear them arguing through the door."

"What were they arguing about?"

"Money, mostly. Ethan was saying something about how they needed to restructure the business, bring in someone who understood finance better. Milo was saying he understood it just fine, that he'd been handling everything perfectly." Georgie shook her head. "Milo's voice kept getting louder and louder. At one point he said something like, 'I made you. Without me, you'd still be sketching in your mother's basement.'"

"What did Ethan say?"

"He got real quiet. Then he said, 'Maybe it's time we found out if that's true.' That's when I made some noise with the vacuum, so they'd know I was there. They stopped arguing right away."

I absorbed this. More evidence that the relationship between the two men had been deteriorating.

"Did you tell the police this?"

"Detective Keller asked me some questions, yeah. I told her they argued sometimes, but I didn't go into detail." She looked uncomfortable. "I don't like gossiping about the residents. People deserve their privacy."

"Of course. I understand."

"But this is different, isn't it? This is murder." She said the word quietly, like she was afraid someone might hear. "I've been thinking about it a lot. About whether I should have said more."

"You can always call Detective Keller back, tell her what you told me."

"Maybe I will." She finished her coffee and stood up. "I should get to work. These apartments won't clean themselves."

"Georgie, one more thing. That day, the day Ethan died. Were you working here?"

"No, that was a Tuesday. I clean this building on Mondays, Wednesdays, and Fridays. I was working at another property that day."

"Do you know who was here? Who might have seen something?"

She thought about it. "Jerry works nights, so he wouldn't have been on until six. Chelsea would have been in her office. Melanie at the front desk, but you know her, she's in her own world half the time. Walter on the door." She ticked them off on her fingers. "Maintenance was here that day too. I remember because Chelsea mentioned they were fixing the elevator on three."

"Maintenance," I repeated. "Who was that?"

"Could have been any of them. We've got a rotating crew. Why?"

"Just trying to get a picture of who was in the building."

Georgie gave me a long look. "Miss Dora Lee, you be careful. If someone did kill that boy, they're dangerous. I don't want to be cleaning your apartment and find you..." She couldn't finish the sentence.

"I'm always careful, dear."

"Hmm." She didn't look convinced. "I'm going to start in the bathroom, work my way out. You just go about your business."

For the next hour, I sat at my sewing table working on Mrs. Noble's alterations while Georgie cleaned. The familiar sounds were soothing. The vacuum, the spray bottle, her humming along to whatever was playing in her earbuds.

When she finished, she came to find me.

"All done. I put fresh sheets on your bed and clean towels in the bathroom."

"Thank you, Georgie. What do I owe you?"

"The building pays me, remember? You don't owe me anything."

"Then this is just because I appreciate you." I pressed two twenties into her hand.

"Miss Dora Lee, you don't have to—"

"I know I don't have to. I want to. Get yourself something nice, or put it toward Jesse's trouble fund."

She laughed and tucked the money into her pocket. "Thank you. You're too good to me."

"You work hard. You deserve it."

After she left, I pulled out my legal pad and added the new information:

NEW INFORMATION FROM GEORGIE:
- Week before murder: big argument about restructuring business
- Ethan wanted someone who "understood finance better"
- Milo said "I made you. Without me, you'd still be sketching in your mother's basement"
- Ethan responded: "Maybe it's time we found out if that's true"
- Relationship clearly deteriorating before the murder
- Milo felt unappreciated, threatened by potential changes

I sat back, tapping my pen against the pad.

Everything pointed to Milo. The motive was clear, the opportunity was there, and he had the access. But something still nagged at me.

If Milo had killed Ethan in a fit of rage or calculated revenge, why was he so desperate for people to believe he was innocent? Why come to my apartment drunk and emotional, looking for someone to talk to?

Unless he was just a very good actor.

Or unless someone wanted it to look like Milo did it.

What if this wasn't about Milo at all? What if someone had killed Ethan and deliberately made it look like Milo was the obvious suspect?

"Pippa, I think I might be looking at this all wrong."

She opened one eye, then closed it again.

I needed to think about who else benefited from Ethan's death. And who might want to frame Milo in the process.

Lawrence Jung, the rival designer. He'd get rid of his competition and potentially discredit another designer at the same time.

Jamie Patton. She was angry at Ethan, but would she have the know-how to stage something like this?

Or maybe someone I hadn't even considered yet. Someone still lurking in the shadows.

I looked at the clock. It was almost noon. Time to open the shop.

But first, I needed to talk to someone who might have a different perspective on all of this.

I needed to talk to Mel Tanner.

Chapter Nine

Getting in touch with Mel Tanner wasn't as easy as just calling him up. The man was a legend in the fashion world, and legends didn't just answer their phones for anyone.

But I had an advantage. I'd known Mel for over forty years.

I pulled out my ancient address book, the one with the worn leather cover and pages yellowed with age. There, under T, was Mel's information. Three crossed-out phone numbers and addresses, and finally, his current contact information scribbled in pencil.

I dialed the number on my landline.

It rang four times before a crisp voice answered. "Tanner Studios."

"Hello, this is Dora Lee Griffen calling for Mel."

"I'm sorry, Mr. Tanner is very busy. If you'd like to schedule an appointment—"

"Tell him Dora Lee Griffen is calling about Ethan Kemper."

There was a pause. "One moment please."

I was put on hold, some classical music playing softly. I waited, watching Pippa snooze on the couch.

After about three minutes, the line clicked.

"Dora Lee Griffen. Now that's a name I haven't heard in a while." Mel's voice was exactly as I remembered it, smooth, cultured, with just a hint of condescension that he probably didn't even know was there.

"Hello, Mel. It's been too long."

"It has. What, five years? Six?"

"Something like that. How have you been?"

"Busy as ever. Three collections in production, a retrospective at the Met next spring. You know how it is." He paused. "Or maybe you don't anymore. I heard your shop is quiet these days."

There was the Mel I remembered. Always had to get a little dig in.

"I keep busy enough. I'm calling about Ethan Kemper."

His tone shifted immediately, becoming somber. "Terrible thing. Just terrible. That boy had so much potential. I was mentoring him, you know."

"I heard. He must have learned a lot from you."

"He was a sponge. Absorbed everything. Reminded me of myself at that age, actually. Hungry, ambitious, willing to do whatever it took to succeed." There was genuine sadness in his voice. "I can't believe he's gone."

"Mel, I need to ask you some questions. About Ethan, about his work, about the people around him."

"Why? What's your interest in this?"

"He lived in my building. I'd gotten to know him a little. And I have some concerns about how he died."

"The police said it was an accident."

"The police are being careful about what they say publicly. But they're investigating it as a murder."

Silence on the other end. Then: "Murder. Jesus. Do they know who did it?"

"Not yet. That's why I'm calling. You knew Ethan better than most. Who would want him dead?"

Another pause. I could almost hear him thinking, weighing his words.

"Can I be frank with you, Dora Lee?"

"Please."

"Ethan made enemies. He was brilliant, but he wasn't always ethical. He took credit for other people's work. He made promises he didn't keep. He burned bridges." Mel sighed. "I tried to counsel him, told him that talent alone wasn't enough. You need integrity too. But he didn't listen."

"Did you know he was stealing designs from his interns?"

"I suspected. Nothing I could prove, but yes. That's part of why I was keeping close to him. I thought maybe I could steer him toward better practices." He laughed bitterly. "Clearly I failed."

"What about Lawrence Jung?"

"What about him?"

"I heard he's in town. Meeting with Milo about the brand."

"Of course he is. Lawrence is a vulture. He circles anything that looks weak or vulnerable." Mel's voice hardened. "And before you ask, yes, I think Lawrence could absolutely kill someone if it served his purposes."

This got my attention. "Really?"

"Lawrence Jung is one of the most ruthless people I've ever met in this industry, and that's saying something. He's been trying to take down Ethan for years. Always coming in second place, always just behind. It ate at him."

"Ate at him enough to commit murder?"

"I don't know. Maybe." Mel paused. "But here's what I do know. Lawrence was in town the day Ethan died. I saw him that afternoon at a fabric supplier's showroom. Around three o'clock, maybe three-thirty."

My pulse quickened. That was right in the middle of the time-of-death window.

"Are you sure?"

"Positive. We had a brief conversation. He was very interested in when Ethan's fashion show was scheduled. Asked a lot of questions about the collection, about Milo's role in the company. It struck me as odd at the time."

"Did you tell the police this?"

"No one's asked me. Should I?"

"Yes. Definitely yes."

"I'll call that detective whose card I have. Keller, I think her name was." He cleared his throat. "Dora Lee, there's something else you should know. About a month ago, Ethan came to me upset. He said he'd caught Lawrence trying to bribe one of his interns for sketches and design notes."

"What did he do about it?"

"He confronted Lawrence. Threatened to go public with it, ruin his reputation. Lawrence backed off, but Ethan said the look in his eyes was..." Mel trailed off. "He said it was murderous. Those were his exact words. 'Mel, the look he gave me was murderous.'"

I was scribbling notes as fast as I could on a scrap of paper.

"Did Ethan seem afraid?"

"Not afraid, exactly. More angry. Indignant. You know how young people are, they think they're invincible." The sadness was back in his voice. "I should have taken it more seriously. Should have warned him to be more careful."

"You couldn't have known, Mel."

"Maybe. Maybe not." He was quiet for a moment. "There's one more thing. That model, Jamie Patton. She came to my studio about two weeks ago, asking if I'd hire her. She spent most of the meeting complaining about Ethan, saying terrible things about him."

"What kind of things?"

"That he was a fraud, that he'd stolen everything from other people, that he didn't deserve his success. She was very bitter, very angry. It was actually quite uncomfortable."

"Did you hire her?"

"God no. I don't need that kind of energy in my studio. But what struck me was how obsessed she seemed. She kept bringing the conversation back to Ethan, over and over. It wasn't healthy."

"Do you think she could have done it?"

"I think a scorned woman with nothing to lose is capable of anything." He paused. "But honestly? My money's on Lawrence. The man has the means, the motive, and the complete lack of conscience necessary to pull off something like this."

We talked for a few more minutes, mostly catching up on mutual acquaintances and changes in the industry. Before we hung up, Mel made me promise to stay in touch.

"You were one of the good ones, Dora Lee. The industry needs more people with actual integrity."

"Coming from you, I'll take that as a compliment."

He laughed. "It was meant as one. Be careful, alright? If you're poking around in a murder investigation, you could be putting yourself in danger."

"I'm just a harmless old lady, Mel."

"Balderdash. You've never been harmless a day in your life."

After we hung up, I sat staring at my notes. Lawrence Jung had been in the city during the murder. He had motive, professional jealousy that had festered for years. He'd tried to steal from Ethan before and been threatened with exposure. And according to Mel, he was ruthless enough to kill.

And then there was Jamie, whose obsession with Ethan seemed to have consumed her. Bitter enough to bad-mouth him all over town, angry enough to make people uncomfortable.

Both of them had stronger motives than I'd initially thought.

I looked at my watch. Nearly one o'clock. I needed to get to the shop, but first I wanted to add all of this to my notes at home.

I pulled out my legal pad and created a new section:

LAWRENCE JUNG - STRONGER SUSPECT:
- In NYC the day of murder (confirmed by Mel, around 3-3:30pm)
- History of professional rivalry with Ethan
- Always second place, which "ate at him" (per Mel)
- Tried to bribe Ethan's intern for designs/sketches
- Ethan threatened to expose him publicly
- Ethan said Lawrence gave him a "murderous look"
- Mel says Lawrence is "ruthless" and "capable of anything"
- Circling the brand now like a vulture
- Has means, motive, and "complete lack of conscience"

JAMIE PATTON - MORE OBSESSED THAN BITTER:
- Went to Mel's studio 2 weeks before murder
- Spent whole meeting complaining about Ethan
- Called him a fraud, said he didn't deserve success
- Kept bringing conversation back to Ethan obsessively
- Mel found it "uncomfortable" and "unhealthy"
- Mel: "scorned woman with nothing to lose is capable of anything"

I sat back and looked at what I'd written. Milo still had motive and opportunity, but now Lawrence and Jamie looked just as guilty. Maybe more so.

"Come on, Pippa. Time to go to work."

She hopped down from the couch, and I clipped on her leash. As we rode the elevator down, I thought about what Mel had said about Lawrence being in the city that afternoon.

If Lawrence had killed Ethan, how would he have gotten access to the gym? He didn't live in the building. Someone would have seen him.

Unless he had help.

Or unless he'd found a way in that didn't require going through the lobby.

The service entrance. The same one Milo could have used.

When we reached the lobby, I made a detour. Instead of heading straight outside, I walked toward the back of the building where the service entrance was located.

Walter called after me. "Miss Dora Lee? You okay?"

"Just fine, dear. Thought I'd take a different route today."

The service entrance was at the end of a hallway that also led to the maintenance office, the storage rooms, and the gym. I pushed through the door and found myself in an alley.

There was no security camera visible, at least not from here. And the door had a standard push-bar exit, which meant it could be opened from inside without a key, but...

I examined the outside of the door. There was a keycard reader. So, you needed a resident keycard to get in from outside.

But what if someone had propped it open? Or what if someone inside had let them in?

"Miss Dora Lee?"

I turned to find Chelsea, the building manager, standing in the alley entrance with a concerned look on her face.

"What are you doing back here?"

I let my shoulders slump and put a confused expression on my face. "Oh dear. I got all turned around. I was trying to go outside and somehow ended up back here." I looked around the alley as if seeing it for the first time. "Where am I?"

Chelsea's expression softened immediately, concern replacing suspicion. "You're at the service entrance, in the back alley. Come on, let me walk you back through."

"Oh, thank you, dear. These hallways all look the same sometimes."

She took my arm gently, guiding me back through the door and into the building. "You're okay, Miss Dora Lee. We're just going to go back through the lobby and out the front door. That's where you usually go, right?"

"Yes, yes. The front door. With Walter." I shuffled along beside her, moving slowly. "I don't know what happened. One minute I knew where I was going, the next..."

"It happens. The building can be confusing." Chelsea kept her hand on my elbow, steering me carefully down the hallway. "You're going to your shop, right?"

"Yes, my shop. Down the block."

"Okay, let's get you outside and pointed in the right direction."

As we walked through the lobby, I saw Walter notice us. His face showed concern.

"Everything alright?" he called.

"Just fine, Walter," Chelsea said. "Miss Dora Lee took a wrong turn. I'm just making sure she gets outside safely."

"You want me to walk her to her shop?" Walter asked.

"Oh no, no," I said quickly. "I'll be just fine once I'm outside. I know the way from there. It's just these hallways that confused me."

Chelsea walked me all the way to the front entrance. "You're sure you're okay? I could call someone for you."

"I'm perfectly fine, dear. Just a silly old woman who can't find her way around her own building." I patted her hand. "Thank you for your help."

"Of course. And Miss Dora Lee? Maybe stick to the main hallways from now on? The back areas can be a bit confusing."

"Good advice. I will."

She held the door open for me, and Pippa and I stepped out into the afternoon sunshine. As we walked toward the shop, I allowed myself a small smile.

Chelsea had completely bought the confused old lady act. Which meant I'd successfully scoped out the service entrance without raising any real suspicions.

The door required a keycard from the outside. But it could be propped open, or someone from inside could let a visitor in. And there were no security cameras visible in that alley.

Lawrence Jung could have gotten into the building without anyone at the front desk seeing him.

So, could anyone else, for that matter.

"Pippa," I said as I unlocked the shop door, "this case is getting more complicated by the minute."

She wagged her tail and trotted to her window bed.

I hung up my coat and got to work, but my mind kept circling back to that service entrance and all the possibilities it represented.

Someone had killed Ethan Kemper. And they'd been smart enough to do it in a way that left multiple suspects and very few answers.

But they'd made one mistake.

They'd done it in my building.

And I was going to figure out who they were.

Chapter Ten

The afternoon at the shop was quiet, which suited me fine. I had work to do.

I spread the emerald green silk-wool blend across my cutting table, smoothing it carefully. The fabric was even more beautiful than I'd remembered, the way it caught the light making it seem almost alive.

I'd already drafted the pattern based on my customer's measurements and the design we'd discussed. Now came the satisfying part, cutting the fabric, watching the pieces take shape.

Pippa dozed in her window bed while I worked, the steady snip-snip of my fabric scissors the only sound in the shop. I cut carefully, precisely, each piece exactly as it needed to be. There was something meditative about this process, the way it required complete focus and left no room for mistakes.

I was pinning the bodice pieces together when the bell over the door chimed.

"Well, if it isn't my favorite recluse," Viola's voice rang out.

I looked up to see her standing in the doorway, impeccably dressed as always in a tailored pantsuit in dove gray with a silk blouse the color of champagne.

"Viola! What brings you by?"

"Can't a friend stop in for a visit?" She walked over to examine my work. "Oh, that's gorgeous. What are you making?"

"Cocktail dress for a customer. She has an event in six weeks."

"The color is divine. And this fabric..." She ran her fingers over it. "Goldstein's?"

"Where else?"

She laughed. "Morris does get the best stuff." She wandered around the shop, looking at the displays. "You know, you really should update your window arrangement. Maybe add some drama, make people stop and look."

"I'm doing fine, Vi."

"Besides," I added, gesturing toward the window where Pippa was curled up in her bed, "Pippa makes plenty of people stop and look. With those ears, everyone loves Pippa."

Viola followed my gaze and laughed. "Well, you're not wrong about that. Those ears are certainly memorable." She smiled fondly at my sleeping dog. "Maybe you should put her in all your marketing materials."

"She'd love that. More attention for her."

"I'm serious, Dora Lee. You have beautiful pieces, but nobody knows they're here. You need to market yourself better."

This was classic Viola. Always trying to fix things, always offering advice whether asked for or not. Part of me appreciated her concern. Another part bristled at the implication that I didn't know how to run my own business.

"I'll take that under consideration."

"I know, I know. I'm just saying." She settled into one of my customer chairs with a sigh. "Actually, I did have a reason for stopping by. Besides just seeing your lovely face, of course."

"Oh?"

"I heard something today that I thought you might find interesting. Given your curiosity about the Ethan Kemper situation."

I set down my pins and gave her my full attention. "What did you hear?"

"You know Jamie Patton? That model who used to work for Ethan?"

"I know of her."

"Well, she had an audition this morning at Bergdorf's. They're looking for models for their fall campaign." Viola leaned forward conspiratorially. "Apparently she had an absolute meltdown. Started crying in the middle of the audition, then got angry and started ranting about how the industry was unfair and how talented people get destroyed while frauds get celebrated."

"Oh my."

"It gets better. She specifically mentioned Ethan by name. Said something like, 'People like Ethan Kemper ruin careers and nobody cares, but now that he's dead everyone wants to act like he was a saint.'" Viola shook her head. "The casting director was horrified. They escorted her out."

I absorbed this, my mind working. "Who told you this?"

"Elise Golding. She was there for the same audition. We had lunch after and she couldn't stop talking about it." Viola studied her manicured nails. "The girl is clearly unstable. Obsessed with Ethan even after he's gone."

"That's concerning."

"Concerning? Dora Lee, it's downright suspicious. If you ask me, the police should be looking very closely at Miss Jamie Patton." She stood up, walking over to the window where Pippa was sleeping. "A woman scorned and all that."

"The police are investigating everyone, I'm sure."

"Are they though?" Viola turned to face me. "From what I hear, they're focusing most of their attention on Milo. Which makes sense, I suppose. He had the most obvious motive."

"What makes you say that?"

"Oh, come on. His best friend dies and he immediately takes over the brand? Plus, all those arguments they'd been having?" She shrugged. "If I were the police, I'd be looking at him too."

I went back to pinning my fabric pieces, trying to keep my expression neutral. "I suppose."

"But between you and me, I think Jamie is just as likely. Maybe more so." Viola came back to sit down. "Women can be vicious when they feel wronged. And that girl felt very wronged."

"Have you met her? Jamie, I mean?"

"Once or twice at industry events. She's beautiful, obviously, but there's something desperate about her. Like she's always trying too hard, you know?" Viola crossed her legs. "And now with this tantrum at Bergdorf's, she's basically blacklisted herself from major campaigns. Her career is over."

"That seems harsh."

"That's the industry, darling. One wrong move and you're done." She checked her watch. "I should get going. I have a meeting with a new fabric supplier in an hour."

"Thanks for stopping by, Vi."

"Of course." She paused at the door. "Dora Lee, you are being careful, aren't you? Asking questions about a murder investigation?"

"I'm just a curious old lady. Nobody pays attention to me."

"Hmm." She didn't look convinced. "Well, stay safe. I'd hate to lose my best friend."

After she left, I stood at my cutting table, thinking about what she'd said. Jamie's public meltdown certainly made her look unstable.

And the obsessive quality that Mel had mentioned seemed to be escalating.

But something about Viola's visit bothered me. The way she'd steered the conversation so deliberately toward Jamie, emphasizing how suspicious the model was. The way she'd mentioned Milo only to then redirect back to Jamie being "just as likely, maybe more so."

It felt calculated.

I shook my head. I was being paranoid. Viola was my friend. She was just sharing gossip, the way friends did.

Still.

I pulled out a scrap of paper and made a note to add to my legal pad at home: Viola pushing suspicion toward Jamie. Why?

"I'm overthinking this, aren't I, Pippa?"

She opened one eye, then closed it again.

I went back to work on the green dress, but part of my mind stayed on that conversation. On the way Viola had presented the information. On the timing of her visit.

On the fact that she seemed very invested in making sure I suspected Jamie.

The question was: why?

Chapter Eleven

That evening, after I'd locked up the shop and returned home, I couldn't stop thinking about that apartment on the fifth floor. There might still be evidence inside. Evidence that could point to the real killer.

I sat in my reading chair with my legal pad, Pippa curled up at my feet.

The problem was obvious: how does an old lady get into someone's apartment without anyone noticing?

The answer was equally obvious: she uses the building's secrets.

I'd grown up in this hotel, spent my childhood exploring every nook and cranny. I knew things about this building that even the current owners didn't know. Things that had been sealed up or forgotten over the decades.

Like the dumbwaiter system.

Most of the dumbwaiters had been removed when the building was converted to apartments, but not all of them. Some had simply been sealed over, hidden behind new walls and forgotten. As a child, I'd mapped out every single one, creating my own secret highway through the building.

The question was: was there still a dumbwaiter that connected to the fifth floor?

I went to my bedroom closet and pulled out an old hatbox from the top shelf. Inside, beneath some vintage hats I never wore anymore, was a rolled-up piece of paper yellowed with age.

My childhood map of the Royal Griffen Hotel.

I spread it out on my dining table, smoothing the creases carefully. There, in my ten-year-old handwriting, were all the secret passages I'd discovered. The dumbwaiters, the service stairs, the utility access panels.

I traced my finger along the fifth floor. There. Apartment 5C, which had been two rooms back when this was a hotel. One of those rooms had contained a dumbwaiter that connected to the fourth floor below and the sixth floor above.

If I could access the dumbwaiter from the sixth floor, I could lower myself down to the fifth. The opening would be in what was probably now a closet or pantry area.

It was risky. Dangerous, even. The dumbwaiter shaft was over seventy years old, and I had no idea if the mechanisms still worked or if the shaft was even intact.

But I had to know what was in that apartment.

"Don't look at me like that, Pippa."

She tilted her head, ears flopping.

"I know it's crazy. But I'm going to do it anyway."

The question was when. I needed to know Milo would be away. Breaking into an occupied apartment was far more dangerous than breaking into an empty one.

I thought about what I'd overheard, what I knew about his schedule. The next day at the shop, I kept my ears open. Sure enough, I overheard two customers discussing an upcoming industry showcase at the Bowery Hotel this weekend, a major event that would draw all the designers.

If Milo was working with Lawrence now, he'd likely attend.

I'd have to wait a few days, but it would be worth it to know the apartment was empty.

For now, I needed to plan. Study my map. Make sure I had everything I needed.

Three days later, on Saturday evening, I saw my opportunity. I was closing up the shop when I spotted Milo in the lobby, dressed in an expensive suit, talking to Lawrence Jung. They were heading out together, clearly on their way to an event.

"We'll be back late," I heard Milo say to Walter. "Don't wait up."

Perfect.

I went upstairs, fed Pippa, and waited. At two in the morning, the building was silent. Most residents were asleep, and Jerry would be dozing in the office.

I dressed in all black: leggings, a long-sleeved shirt, and soft-soled shoes. I felt ridiculous, like I was playing dress-up as a cat burglar, but practicality won over vanity.

I took the stairs down to the sixth floor, moving as quietly as possible. The sixth floor hallway was silent, all the doors closed.

According to my map, the dumbwaiter access should be in the utility closet at the end of the hall. I tried the door handle.

Locked.

Of course it was locked. But I'd come prepared. From my pocket, I pulled out a set of old skeleton keys that had belonged to my father. He'd kept them even after the hotel was sold, and I'd inherited them when he died.

The third key worked. The door opened with a soft click, and I slipped inside, closing it behind me.

The utility closet was cramped and smelled of cleaning supplies. I pulled out my phone and used the flashlight to look around.

There. On the back wall, partially hidden behind a shelf unit, was the outline of the old dumbwaiter door.

I moved the shelf as quietly as I could, wincing at every scrape and squeak. Behind it was the dumbwaiter door, sealed with several layers of paint.

I pulled out a utility knife I'd brought and carefully scored around the edges of the door. The paint cracked and peeled away. After a few minutes of work, I was able to pry the door open.

The shaft beyond was dark and smelled of dust and age. I shone my phone light down and could see the dumbwaiter platform about three feet below, covered in decades of grime.

"Here goes nothing," I whispered.

I sat on the edge of the opening and lowered myself down onto the platform. It creaked ominously under my weight, and for a terrifying moment I thought it might give way. But it held.

The pulley system was still intact, though the ropes looked ancient and frayed in places. I tested them gently, pulling on the rope that would lower the platform.

It moved. Slowly, with lots of squeaking and groaning, but it moved.

I lowered myself down one floor, my heart pounding the entire time. If the rope snapped, I'd fall straight down the shaft. If the platform gave way, same result. If someone heard me and called security, I'd have a lot of explaining to do.

It almost felt like I was that mischievous ten-year-old girl again, only with a lot more aches and pains.

But I'd spent my whole life being underestimated. It was time to use that to my advantage.

The platform jerked to a stop at the fifth floor. I could see the outline of another sealed dumbwaiter door in front of me. This one was easier to open from inside, just a simple latch that slid to the side.

I pushed the door open and found myself looking into a dark closet.

I climbed out as quietly as possible and stood still, listening. The apartment was silent. No sounds of Milo returning early.

I was in.

I moved through the apartment slowly, using my phone's flashlight sparingly. The place was a mess, not from any police search but from how Ethan and Milo lived. Clothes everywhere, dishes in the sink, papers scattered across every surface.

The living room had clearly been their workspace. There were two desks pushed against opposite walls, each covered with sketches, fabric swatches, and notes.

I went to Ethan's desk first. His sketches were beautiful, I had to admit. Bold lines, interesting silhouettes. But as I looked through them, I started to notice something odd.

Some of the sketches had notations in a different handwriting. Corrections, suggestions, and completely different design elements added in the margins. The handwriting was small and precise, very different from Ethan's flowing script.

I took photos of several pages with my phone.

Moving to Milo's desk, I found more of the same. But here, the sketches were more complete, more refined. And many of them looked suspiciously similar to the ones on Ethan's desk that had been "corrected."

So, Milo had been contributing more than just business management. He'd been actively designing, maybe even fixing Ethan's work.

I moved to the bedroom next. Two twin beds, one on each side of the room. Very college dormitory. Ethan's side was messy, clothes piled on the floor. Milo's side was neat, almost obsessively so.

On Milo's nightstand was a stack of fashion magazines. I flipped through them and found several with pages dog-eared or marked. All of them featured Lawrence Jung's work.

Interesting, but not necessarily incriminating. Designers studied each other's work all the time.

Then I noticed something sticking out from under Milo's mattress. Just a corner of paper.

I pulled it out and found myself holding a letter.

It was addressed to Milo, postmarked two weeks before Ethan's death. No return address.

I unfolded it and read:

We need to talk. Meet me at the usual place Tuesday at 2. Come alone. Don't tell E.

It was signed with just the initial "L."

My heart raced. L for Lawrence? The letter was dated the day Ethan died. Tuesday. And it said to meet at 2, right when the argument in the lobby had happened.

I took photos of the letter from every angle, making sure to capture the postmark and the handwriting.

This was it. This was evidence that Milo had been in contact with Lawrence, that they'd planned to meet the day of the murder.

I kept searching, finding more fashion magazines featuring Lawrence's work, more notes in margins about design techniques. Milo had clearly been studying Lawrence Jung intensively.

In the kitchen, I found a calendar on the refrigerator. Most of the dates were filled with appointments, fittings, meetings. But Tuesday, the day Ethan died, had been marked through with a big X. And in the corner, in tiny letters: "2pm - LJ"

I photographed that too.

I was about to leave when I noticed a closet I hadn't checked yet. Inside were racks of clothes, mostly men's suits and jackets. I recognized several pieces from Viola's collections.

And then, at the back of the closet, I found something that made my blood run cold.

A gym bag. Inside were workout clothes, still damp and smelling of sweat. And tucked into the side pocket was a keycard.

Not just any keycard. A maintenance keycard for the building.

The kind that would open any door, including the service entrance. Including the gym.

I photographed everything, then carefully put it all back exactly as I'd found it.

I'd seen enough. More than enough.

I made my way back to the closet with the dumbwaiter, climbed back onto the platform, and slowly, carefully, pulled myself back up to the sixth floor.

By the time I made it back to my apartment, it was nearly four in the morning. I was exhausted, covered in dust and grime, and my hands were shaking from adrenaline.

But I had evidence.

Milo had been in contact with Lawrence Jung. They'd planned to meet the day of the murder. And Milo had access to a maintenance keycard that would have allowed him to move through the building undetected.

But why? What was the connection between Milo and Lawrence?

I sat at my dining table and looked through all the photos I'd taken. The letter, the calendar, the sketches, the magazines, the keycard.

And suddenly, it clicked.

What if Milo hadn't killed Ethan alone? What if Lawrence had been involved?

What if they'd planned it together?

Lawrence wanted Ethan out of the way, wanted to be the rising star without competition. Milo wanted to step out of Ethan's shadow, wanted credit for his own work.

They both had motive. They both had opportunity.

And if they'd worked together, they could have created the perfect murder.

Milo lures Ethan to the gym, maybe says he wants to talk, wants to apologize for their fight. Lawrence gets into the building through the service entrance using the keycard. Together, they trap Ethan in the sauna.

Then Milo makes a big show of going for a run, establishing his alibi. Lawrence disappears. And Ethan dies.

It fit. It all fit.

But I needed proof. Real proof, not just circumstantial evidence and theories.

I needed to talk to Lawrence Jung.

Chapter Twelve

Every muscle ached from my dumbwaiter adventure, and I had bruises forming on my shins that would be spectacular by tomorrow.

"Getting too old for this nonsense," I muttered as I shuffled to the bathroom. "I'm sure to feel worse tomorrow."

Pippa followed me, her nails clicking on the hardwood floor. She tilted her head and gave me a look that clearly said, "You did this to yourself."

"I know, I know. Don't judge me."

After a long hot shower that helped ease some of the soreness, I got dressed in comfortable clothes: wide-leg linen pants in a dusty rose color, a cream silk blouse, and a long chunky cardigan in variegated pinks and oranges. My body might hurt, but I could still look fabulous.

I fed Pippa and made myself coffee, then sat down to review the photos from last night. The letter signed "L," the calendar notation "2pm - LJ," the maintenance keycard. It all pointed to a connection between Milo and Lawrence Jung.

The question was: how did I get close to Lawrence Jung?

I couldn't just walk up to a famous designer and start asking questions about murder. He'd either laugh me off or call security.

But maybe I didn't need to approach him directly. Maybe I just needed to observe him, see what he was up to, figure out if he was acting guilty.

According to what Ellie had said, Lawrence was meeting with Milo about the brand. And Viola had mentioned seeing him at a fabric supplier's showroom.

Lawrence Jung would be doing what any designer would do after acquiring a promising brand: sourcing materials, meeting with manufacturers, planning the next collection.

Which meant he'd likely be in the fashion district.

"Come on, Pippa. We're going hunting."

She wagged her tail and did a little spin, which was her way of saying she was excited.

I decided to start at Goldstein's. Morris knew everyone in the industry and loved to gossip. If Lawrence Jung had been sniffing around for fabrics, Morris would know about it.

We took a taxi down to the fabric district, and Pippa spent the entire ride with her head out the window, ears flapping in the wind like a pair of flags.

"Careful, Miss," the driver said, laughing. "She might take flight with those ears."

"She's tried," I said. "Haven't you, Pip?"

She pulled her head back in and sneezed, which made the driver laugh even harder.

When we arrived at Goldstein's, Morris was helping another customer, so I browsed the new arrivals. Some gorgeous raw silk had come in, and I was seriously considering buying some even though I had no immediate use for it.

That was the problem with being a fabric addict. There was always something irresistible.

"Dora Lee!" Morris called out when his customer left. "Back so soon? You go through that green silk already?"

"Not yet, Morris. I'm actually here on a fishing expedition."

"Oh?" His eyes lit up. He loved a good intrigue. "What kind of fish are we after?"

"Lawrence Jung. Has he been in recently?"

Morris's expression shifted. "Jung. Yes, he was here yesterday. Bought up half my stock of Italian wool. Very specific about what he wanted." He leaned on the counter. "Why do you want to know about Jung?"

"Just curious. He's taking over a brand and I wondered what direction he's going with it."

"The Kemper brand, you mean." Morris shook his head. "Terrible thing, that boy dying. Such talent." He studied me. "You live in that building, don't you? Where it happened?"

"I do."

"And now you're asking about Jung." He tapped his nose knowingly. "You think he had something to do with it."

"I don't think anything. I'm just a nosy old lady."

"Hmm." He didn't believe me for a second. "Well, nosy old lady, Jung is doing a presentation this afternoon at the Madison

Design Center. Three o'clock. He's showing the direction he wants to take the brand."

"A presentation?"

"By invitation only. Very exclusive. All the major buyers and fashion press." Morris grinned. "But I happen to have an extra invitation. My nephew was supposed to go with me, but he came down with the flu."

"Morris Goldstein, you are a treasure."

"I know, I know. Just remember me when you solve your murder mystery."

He handed me an elegant cream-colored invitation with raised lettering. Very fancy.

Pippa had been sitting patiently during this conversation, but now she stood up and offered Morris her paw.

"Oh, look at this! What a lady!" Morris came around the counter and shook her paw solemnly. "You are a very proper dog, Miss Pippa."

She wagged her tail, then sat back and raised both paws in the air.

"She begs!" Morris laughed with delight. He reached under the counter and pulled out a small tin. "I keep dog biscuits for the fashion dogs. Here you go, sweetheart."

Pippa caught the biscuit mid-air and chomped it down, then immediately went back to begging.

"Just one," I said firmly. "She'll con you out of the whole tin if you let her."

"Smart girl." Morris gave her one more, then put the tin away. "She knows how to work a room."

After thanking Morris profusely, Pippa and I headed back home. The presentation was at three, which gave me several hours to prepare.

And by prepare, I meant figure out how to look like I belonged at an exclusive fashion industry event while also being old and forgettable enough that Lawrence Jung wouldn't pay attention to me.

Back at the apartment, I went through my closet carefully. I needed something that said "fashion insider" but also "harmless elderly woman." Not an easy combination.

Finally, I settled on a vintage Chanel-style suit in black and cream tweed. It was classic, elegant, and just dated enough to make me look like someone who'd been in the industry for decades. I paired it with my good pearls, low black pumps, and a structured handbag.

I studied myself in the mirror. Perfect. I looked like a retired fashion editor or a wealthy patron of the arts. Exactly the kind of person who might be invited to a presentation like this.

"What do you think, Pippa?"

She tilted her head, considering, then wagged her tail.

"I'll take that as approval. Now let's get you dressed."

I pulled out one of Pippa's special outfits from her drawer. A little black and white dress that I'd made to coordinate with various outfits of my own, complete with a pearl collar that matched my necklace. She stood patiently while I put it on her, used to being my fashion-coordinated companion.

"Now we're a proper pair."

At two-thirty, I called for a car to take me to the Madison Design Center. Pippa came with me, of course. Fashion people loved dogs, and she was my perfect cover. Nobody suspected a woman with an adorable dog.

The Madison Design Center was a sleek modern building in Midtown, all glass and steel. The lobby was already filling with well-dressed people clutching similar cream-colored invitations.

I showed mine to the woman at the desk, and she checked me off a list.

"Enjoy the presentation, Ms..." She looked at me expectantly.

"Griffen. Dora Lee Griffen."

Her eyes widened, and she actually stood up from her chair. "The Dora Lee Griffen? From the eighties and nineties?"

"That would be me."

"Oh my gosh, I studied your work in design school. Your 1987 collection was revolutionary. The way you incorporated traditional quilting techniques into haute couture? Genius." She was practically glowing. "It's such an honor to meet you." She looked down at Pippa. "And oh my goodness, what a cutie! Look at those ears!"

"Thank you, dear. That's very kind."

"Please, go right up. Third floor, the Anderson Gallery." She was still staring at me with stars in her eyes. "This is honestly the highlight of my week."

I shuffled to the elevator, playing up the old lady act, though inside I was smiling. It was nice to be remembered.

The third floor was packed with industry people. I recognized several faces from over the years, though most were much younger than me. Fashion was a young person's game now.

As soon as I stepped off the elevator, a silver-haired man in an expensive suit turned and did a double-take.

"Dora Lee Griffen? Is that really you?"

"Harold Zimmerman. How are you?"

"I'm wonderful, but more importantly, what are you doing here? I thought you'd retired completely." He came over and took both my hands. "You look fantastic."

"Oh, I still dabble. Small shop, custom work."

"Still too modest, I see." He smiled warmly. "Your work influenced an entire generation of designers. You know that, right?"

Before I could respond, a woman in a striking red pantsuit approached. "Harold, are you monopolizing Dora Lee Griffen?" She extended her hand to me. "Janine Cross, Vogue. I did a retrospective piece on your work about five years ago."

"I remember. It was very flattering."

"It was accurate," she corrected. "Your use of color and texture was decades ahead of its time. Are you working on anything new?"

As we made our way through the crowd, more people noticed me. It was like a ripple effect.

"Is that Dora Lee Griffen?"

"Oh my God, I didn't know she was still in the city."

"Her 1992 runway show is still one of the most talked about in fashion history."

A young man, probably in his late twenties, approached nervously. "Miss Griffen? I'm so sorry to bother you, but I have to tell you that your work inspired me to become a designer. Your book on color theory is my bible."

"That's very sweet of you, dear. What's your name?"

"David Newberry. I have a small line, nothing major yet, but..." He pulled out his phone. "Would you mind if I took a photo? My professors will never believe I met you."

I obliged, and Pippa, sensing an opportunity, immediately sat up and posed as well.

"Oh, what a cutie!"

"She is dressed so cute! Look at her little pearl collar!"

"Those ears! I can't even handle it!"

A woman in an expensive-looking wrap dress actually stopped mid-conversation to crouch down. "You are the most adorable thing I've ever seen."

Pippa, ever the performer, offered her paw.

"And she shakes hands! I'm dying."

I smiled indulgently as we continued through the room. "You're quite popular today, Pippa."

She wagged her tail, clearly pleased with all the attention.

Servers circulated with champagne and tiny canapés. Pippa immediately went into full performance mode, sitting prettily at my feet and looking up with those enormous eyes.

A young waiter stopped. "Oh wow, she matches your outfit! That's incredible. What's her name?"

"Pippa."

"Hi, Pippa!" He bent down to pet her, and she offered him her paw. He shook it, delighted. "Does she do any other tricks?"

"Show him your spin, Pippa."

She stood up and spun in a circle, then sat back down and raised both paws in the air.

The waiter laughed. "That's amazing! Hold on." He disappeared for a moment and came back with a small plate of what looked like fancy cheese cubes. "For the talented lady."

I let Pippa have one cube, which she ate delicately, then went right back to begging.

"Just one more," the waiter said, giving in. "You're too cute."

After he walked away, I bent down to whisper to Pippa. "You're shameless. But effective."

I was accepting a glass of champagne from another server when I heard a familiar voice behind me.

"Dora Lee Griffen. Well, this is a surprise."

I turned to find Viola standing there in a stunning emerald green dress that hugged her figure perfectly. Her expression was curious, with just a hint of suspicion.

"Viola! I didn't expect to see you here."

"I could say the same." She air-kissed both my cheeks. "When did you start attending industry presentations again? You've been practically a hermit for years."

"I got an invitation through Morris Goldstein. His nephew was sick, so I took his spot." I gestured around the room. "It's nice to see what the young designers are up to."

"Hmm." Viola studied me carefully. "And it has nothing to do with the fact that Lawrence Jung is presenting? The same Lawrence Jung who's taking over Ethan Kemper's brand? The same Ethan Kemper who died in your building?"

"That's quite a leap, Vi."

"Is it though?" She sipped her champagne. "You've been asking questions about the murder. Having dinner with me to pump me for information about Milo. And now you show up here, at Lawrence's presentation."

"I'm just a curious old lady."

"Balderdash." She lowered her voice. "Dora Lee, what are you doing? This isn't some game. If someone really did murder that boy, they're dangerous."

"I'm being careful."

"Are you?" She glanced around to make sure no one was listening. "Lawrence Jung is not someone to mess with. He's ruthless, Dora Lee. Absolutely ruthless."

"So, you've said."

"I'm serious. If he even suspects you're investigating him..." She trailed off meaningfully.

Before I could respond, Lawrence himself appeared, moving through the crowd with Milo trailing behind him. When he spotted Viola, his face lit up.

"Viola! I'm so glad you could make it." He kissed her on both cheeks, European-style. "Your opinion means everything to me."

"Lawrence, congratulations on the partnership. Very exciting." She gestured to Milo. "And Milo, of course. How are you holding up?"

Milo's smile was strained. "Fine. Busy, but fine."

"I can imagine." Viola's tone was sympathetic, but her eyes were sharp, assessing. "It must be difficult, continuing without Ethan."

"We're managing," Lawrence said smoothly, answering for Milo. "In fact, I think we're going to create something even better than what Ethan envisioned. No offense to the dead, of course."

The casualness with which he dismissed Ethan made my stomach turn.

Lawrence noticed me for the first time. "And who is this lovely lady?"

"Lawrence, this is Dora Lee Griffen," Viola said. "Dora Lee, Lawrence Jung."

His eyes widened with recognition. "The Dora Lee Griffen? What an honor." He took my hand, his grip firm and confident. "I'm a huge admirer of your work. Your color theory was groundbreaking. I actually have a first edition of your book in my studio."

"You're very kind."

"Are you still designing?"

"Oh, just a small shop. Nothing like what you're doing." I gestured vaguely. "This is very impressive."

"Thank you. It's a labor of love, really. Ethan's death was such a tragedy, but I feel it's my responsibility to carry on his legacy." The words were practiced, smooth.

Viola was watching the interaction carefully, her gaze moving between me and Lawrence.

"How did you two connect?" I asked, looking between Lawrence and Milo. "I imagine it happened quite quickly after Ethan's death."

Milo shifted uncomfortably, but Lawrence answered without hesitation. "Actually, Milo and I had been talking for a while. Hadn't we, Milo?"

Milo nodded. "Yeah. Lawrence had expressed interest in collaborating even before..." He trailed off.

"Before Ethan died," Lawrence finished. "I saw potential in what they were building. When this tragedy happened, I knew I had to step in. The brand was too important to let it die with Ethan."

"How fortunate," Viola said, her tone neutral but her eyes sharp.

"Very fortunate," I agreed, watching both men carefully.

Pippa, who had been sitting quietly at my feet, suddenly stood up and growled. Softly, but definitely a growl.

She never growled.

Lawrence looked down at her, and for just a moment, his pleasant expression slipped. Something cold flickered in his eyes.

Then he smiled. "Cute dog. What's her name?"

"Pippa."

"Well, Pippa doesn't seem to like me very much." He laughed, but it sounded forced.

"She's usually very friendly," I said. "I don't know what's gotten into her."

But I did know. Pippa had good instincts about people. And right now, her instincts were telling her that Lawrence Jung was dangerous.

Viola was watching this exchange with interest. "Animals have excellent instincts," she said casually. "They can sense things we can't."

"Or maybe she just doesn't like my cologne," Lawrence said with another forced laugh. He turned to Milo. "We should mingle. The Neiman's buyers are here."

"Of course." Milo looked at me one more time, something unreadable in his expression, then followed Lawrence into the crowd.

Viola waited until they were out of earshot, then turned to me. "Well, that was interesting."

"What was?"

"The way Lawrence answered for Milo. The way Milo looked like he wanted to say something else. The way your dog growled at Lawrence." She studied me. "You're onto something, aren't you?"

"I don't know what you mean."

"Dora Lee." She took my arm, steering me toward a quieter corner. "We've been friends for over forty years. I know when you're investigating something. What did you find?"

I hesitated. Viola was my friend, but something about this whole situation made me wary. The way she'd been steering suspicion toward Jamie, the way she seemed so invested in directing my investigation.

"I'm just observing," I said carefully. "Trying to understand what happened to that boy."

"And what have you observed?"

"That Lawrence and Milo had a relationship before Ethan died. That Lawrence is very comfortable taking control. That Milo seems..." I searched for the right word. "Trapped."

Viola nodded slowly. "Lawrence has a way of doing that. Taking over, making himself indispensable." She glanced over at where Lawrence was holding court with the buyers. "He's brilliant, but he's also calculating. Everything is a chess move with him."

"Do you think he could have killed Ethan?"

She was quiet for a long moment. "I think Lawrence is capable of a lot of things. But murder?" She shrugged. "That seems extreme, even for him. Though if anyone could plan and execute a perfect murder, it would be Lawrence Jung."

A woman I didn't recognize tapped a microphone at the front of the room.

"Ladies and gentlemen, if you could please take your seats, we're ready to begin."

Everyone moved toward the rows of chairs set up facing a small stage. Viola squeezed my arm.

"Be careful, Dora Lee. Please."

"I will."

She went to sit with a group of buyers near the front. I found a seat in the back, perfect for observing everything.

Pippa settled under my chair and promptly fell asleep. All that begging for treats was exhausting work.

Lawrence Jung took the stage, and the lights dimmed slightly. A large screen behind him lit up with images of sketches and fabric swatches.

"Thank you all for coming," he began, his voice smooth and confident. "Today, I want to share with you the future of the Ethan Kemper brand."

I noticed he said "Ethan Kemper brand" not "Kemper and Savage" or anything that acknowledged Milo's contribution.

Interesting.

"Ethan was a visionary," Lawrence continued. "His work represented a new direction in American fashion. Bold, unapologetic, fearless."

He clicked to the next slide, showing one of Ethan's designs.

"But vision alone isn't enough. Vision needs refinement. Structure. Experience." Another click. "That's what I bring to this partnership. The wisdom of someone who's been doing this for twenty years."

He went on like that for several minutes, praising Ethan while simultaneously positioning himself as the one who would make Ethan's vision actually work. It was masterfully done, and the audience ate it up.

But I kept watching Milo, who stood off to the side of the stage. His face was carefully neutral, but his hands were clenched into fists.

Lawrence showed more slides, talking about the upcoming collection, the marketing strategy, the retail partnerships he'd already secured.

"And none of this would be possible without my partner in this venture, Milo Savage." Lawrence gestured toward Milo, who stepped forward slightly. "Milo worked closely with Ethan and understands the brand DNA better than anyone."

Polite applause. Milo nodded but didn't smile. Under the stage lights, I could see the tension in his jaw, the way his shoulders stayed rigid even as he tried to appear relaxed. His hands were clasped in front of him, knuckles white. When he spoke, his voice was steady enough, but I noticed how he kept swallowing between sentences, like his mouth had gone dry.

He looked like someone barely holding it together. Like the facade might crack at any moment.

"Together," Lawrence said, putting his arm around Milo's shoulders, "we're going to take this brand to heights that Ethan could only dream of."

The presentation continued for another twenty minutes, with Lawrence doing most of the talking and Milo occasionally chiming in with technical details about construction or materials.

It was clear who was the star and who was the supporting player.

When it ended, people swarmed Lawrence with questions and congratulations. Milo drifted to the edge of the crowd, looking lost.

Viola was in the thick of it, talking animatedly with Lawrence and several buyers. She laughed at something he said, touching his arm in that familiar way she had.

They seemed quite comfortable with each other.

I filed that observation away for later.

This was my chance to talk to Milo without Lawrence hovering.

I shuffled over to where he stood, Pippa at my heels.

"Hello again, dear. That was quite a presentation."

He looked down at me, and up close, the deterioration was even more obvious. His eyes were bloodshot, the kind that comes from too many late nights and not enough sleep. There was a tremor in his hands that he tried to hide by shoving them in his pockets. The expensive suit couldn't hide how much weight he'd lost. The fabric bunched slightly at his waist where it should have fit perfectly.

"Thanks." His voice was hoarse, like he'd been shouting. Or crying.

"You must be very excited about this partnership."

"Yeah. Excited." His tone said the opposite. He glanced over his shoulder, checking where Lawrence was, then back to me. There was something desperate in his eyes. Something haunted. "It's everything I wanted, right? To step out of Ethan's shadow. To get credit for my work."

The way he said it didn't sound like victory. It sounded like he was trying to convince himself.

"It's wonderful that you're getting to continue Ethan's work."

Something flashed across his face, pain, sharp and immediate, before he could mask it. His jaw clenched so hard I could see the muscle jump. When he spoke again, his voice was barely above a whisper.

"That's one way to put it."

"Is there another way?"

He looked at me for a long moment, and I saw something in his eyes I recognized from my own mirror during my darkest days. Regret. Deep, soul-crushing regret. His hands came out of his pockets, and I noticed how they shook before he clasped them together.

"Can I ask you something, Miss Dora Lee?"

"Of course."

"When you were starting out as a designer, when you were young and trying to make a name for yourself, did you ever feel like you were invisible?" His voice cracked slightly on the word 'invisible.' "Like no matter how good your work was, nobody saw you?"

"Many times."

"How did you deal with it?" The question came out urgent, almost pleading. Like he needed the answer for more than professional reasons.

"I kept working. I trusted that eventually, the work would speak for itself." I paused, studying his face. "But it sounds like you're not sure the work is being seen, even now."

He laughed bitterly, but the sound was hollow. Empty. "You could say that." He rubbed his face with both hands, and when he dropped them, he looked even more exhausted. "I thought this was what I wanted. But it turns out getting everything you want doesn't always feel the way you thought it would."

The way he said it sent a chill through me. It sounded like a confession of something much darker than career dissatisfaction.

Before I could press further, Lawrence appeared at his elbow.

"Milo, the buyers from Neiman's want to talk timeline." He noticed me again, his smile not quite reaching his eyes. "Miss Griffen, I hope you enjoyed the presentation."

"Very much. You have an impressive vision."

"Thank you." He turned to Milo. "Shall we?"

Milo looked like he wanted to say something more, but he just nodded and let Lawrence steer him away.

I stood there watching them go, my mind working through everything I'd seen and heard.

Lawrence and Milo had known each other before Ethan died. They'd been "talking for a while" about collaboration. Lawrence had moved in immediately after Ethan's death, taking control of the brand.

And Milo, who'd been in Ethan's shadow, was now in Lawrence's shadow.

Unless Milo had traded one shadow for another willingly. Unless this had all been part of a plan.

"Ready to go, Pippa?"

She stood up and stretched, shaking herself awake.

As we made our way to the elevator, I caught sight of Viola still talking with Lawrence. She saw me leaving and raised her hand in a small wave. I waved back.

But something about the whole scene bothered me. The way Viola had been so comfortable with Lawrence, the way she'd warned me away from investigating him, the way she kept redirecting suspicion toward other people.

What did Viola know? And more importantly, what wasn't she telling me?

Chapter Thirteen

My phone woke me before my alarm, buzzing with text after text. I fumbled for my reading glasses.

"What in the world?"

Messages from numbers I didn't recognize, a few I did. All saying the same thing: how wonderful to see me at the presentation, was I coming back to fashion, could they visit my shop?

Word had spread that Dora Lee Griffen was still alive and kicking.

I smiled, setting the phone down. Maybe Viola had been right about marketing myself better. Though this wasn't exactly what I'd had in mind.

After my treadmill session and Pippa's breakfast, I chose my outfit carefully. A flowing maxi dress in shades of purple and blue with a geometric print, long beaded necklace, comfortable ankle boots. If people were coming to see a legend, I might as well look the part.

"Big day ahead, Pippa. We might actually have customers."

She wagged her tail enthusiastically.

At the shop, I barely had the door unlocked before the first person walked in.

"Oh my gosh, you're really here!" A young woman, mid-twenties, perfectly styled, outfit screaming "fashion student." "I saw you yesterday at the presentation and I just had to see your work in person. I'm Zoe. I'm getting my MFA at Parsons."

"Welcome, Zoe. Please, look around."

She moved through the shop like it was a museum, touching fabrics reverently, examining seams with the attention to detail I recognized from my own youth.

"These are all hand-sewn?"

"Every single one."

"The craftsmanship is incredible. We don't see this kind of quality anymore." She held up a jacket I'd finished last month. "Everything is so fast fashion now. Just churn it out, make it cheap, who cares if it falls apart in six months. This is art."

She bought a vintage-style blouse and floated out the door.

But she was just the beginning. Over the next hour, five more people came in. Students, young professionals, a fashion blogger who took approximately fifty photos of the shop and Pippa.

"This is amazing content," the blogger said, crouching for a shot of Pippa in her window bed. "My followers are going to die. Do you have social media? Instagram? TikTok?"

"I have a landline." I had a cell phone too, but it was a fairly simple model. I didn't do all that online stuff. I just preferred the old-fashioned things, retro, the kids called it.

She laughed, then realized I was serious. "Oh. Well, you should really think about getting online. You'd blow up."

I had no idea what "blow up" meant, but I smiled and nodded.

Around eleven, someone walked through the door who made me look twice. Tall, willowy, with dark skin and cheekbones that could cut glass. The kind of face you'd see in Vogue or on a runway.

"Miss Griffen? I hope you don't mind me stopping by. I'm Elise Golding. I saw you at Lawrence's presentation yesterday."

Elise Golding. The model Viola had mentioned.

"Of course, dear. Welcome."

"I heard about this place from Viola actually. She mentioned you'd made custom pieces for her over the years."

"I have. Viola's been a good friend for a long time."

As Elise browsed, Pippa performed her usual routine, offering her paw and spinning for treats.

"She's adorable. Those ears!" Elise laughed. "I saw her yesterday at the presentation. She's quite the scene-stealer." She paused, holding up a dress. "Speaking of that presentation, what did you think?"

"Very polished. Lawrence clearly knows what he's doing."

"He does. Though I have to say, I feel bad for Milo. He looked miserable up there." She turned to look at me. "Did you know Ethan? I worked with him a few times. He was complicated."

"I didn't know him well. Just as a neighbor."

"Right, you live in the building where he died. That must have been awful." She brought the dress to the counter. "The whole thing is so tragic. And weird, you know? The timing of it all."

"What do you mean?"

"Well, Lawrence just happens to swoop in right after Ethan dies? And Milo, who'd been fighting with Ethan constantly, suddenly has a new partner?" She shook her head. "I don't know. It feels too convenient."

"You think Lawrence had something to do with it?"

"I didn't say that." She lowered her voice. "But Lawrence Jung doesn't do anything without a plan. If he saw an opportunity in Ethan's death, he'd take it. That's just who he is."

I rang up her purchase. "Did you ever work with Jamie Patton?"

Her expression shifted. "Jamie. Yeah, we've done a few shows together. Why?"

"I heard she had some trouble at an audition recently."

Elise sighed. "That girl is her own worst enemy. She's talented, beautiful, but she can't get out of her own way. Ever since Ethan dropped her, she's been spiraling."

"Spiraling how?"

"Just bitter. Angry. She shows up to auditions and bad-mouths other designers. Posts vague things on social media about the industry being corrupt." Elise picked up her bag. "Between you and me, I think she needs help. Professional help. The way she talks about Ethan, even now that he's dead, it's not healthy."

"Does she talk about him a lot?"

"Constantly. At a recent audition, she completely fell apart. Started crying about how Ethan ruined her career, then got angry and started yelling. It was uncomfortable to watch." She paused at the door. "I hope the police are looking at her. Because if anyone had a reason to want Ethan dead, it was Jamie."

After Elise left, I stood by the window, watching her disappear down the street. That "recent audition" had to be the Bergdorf's one Viola mentioned. Two people now, Viola and Elise, pointing fingers at Jamie. Almost like they were working from the same script.

Interesting.

The afternoon brought more customers. A few browsers, several sales. Then, around one o'clock, an older woman walked in. Probably in her sixties, impeccably dressed in designer labels that I recognized immediately. Not just expensive. Discerning.

"Dora Lee Griffen." She said it like a statement of fact. "I heard through the grapevine that you were still designing."

"And you are?"

"Patricia Hendricks. We met years ago at a show." She smiled. "You probably don't remember. It was 1987, your collection with the quilting techniques. I was a buyer for Bergdorf's then."

That year, 1987, had been my breakthrough year. "I do remember that show."

"I bought six pieces that season. Still have three of them." She moved through the shop with the practiced eye of someone who'd spent decades evaluating fashion. "This is extraordinary work, Dora Lee. This level of craftsmanship is nearly extinct."

"Thank you."

She pulled out a jacket in deep emerald, examining the seams, the hand-stitching, the way the fabric draped. "Do you know what's happening in fashion right now?"

"I try to keep up."

"Everyone's sick of it. The fast fashion, the disposable clothes, the lack of artistry. There's a hunger for what you do. Real craftsmanship. Bold colors. Joy." She held up the jacket. "This is what people are craving and don't even know it yet."

I watched her carefully. This wasn't just a customer browsing. This was a professional assessing.

"I retired from buying five years ago," Patricia continued, "but I still have connections. Still go to shows. And I'm telling you, Dora Lee, there's a space opening up for exactly what you do." She looked at me directly. "You should do a show."

"A show?"

"Not a huge production. Something intimate. Invite the right people, show a tight collection, remind everyone why your name matters." She pulled out two more pieces, a dress and a skirt. "I'll take these. And I want you to seriously consider what I said."

As I rang up her purchase, Patricia leaned on the counter. "I'm not just being nostalgic. I'm seeing a real shift in the market. The young designers coming up, they're looking backward for inspiration. They're studying people like you. Wouldn't it be something if you showed them how it's actually done?"

"I haven't done a runway show in over a decade."

"So? You think people forgot how?" She smiled. "You're Dora Lee Griffen. You wrote the book on color theory that every design student still reads. Your 1987 collection changed how people thought about traditional techniques in modern fashion. You don't need to prove anything to anyone. But you could if you wanted to."

After she left, I stood at the counter, looking around my shop. The racks of dresses, the displays of jackets and skirts, the fabric waiting to be transformed. I'd been content here, in my small world. Safe.

But Patricia's words had planted something. Not just flattery. A genuine observation about the market, about timing, about opportunity.

Maybe there was more than one mystery to solve.

Around three o'clock, a young man walked in. It took me a moment to place him.

"You're Huck, aren't you? Milo's friend?"

He looked surprised. "Yeah. Have we met?"

"Not officially. I've seen you around the building." I didn't mention the eavesdropping. "What brings you in?"

"I heard about your shop from Milo. He mentioned you made beautiful things." He looked around nervously. "I'm actually looking for a gift. For my mom. Her birthday is coming up."

"How wonderful. Tell me about her. What's her style like?"

"Her style?" He seemed surprised by the question. "Um, she likes colors. Bright things. She's always complaining that everything in stores is black or gray or beige."

"A woman after my own heart." I moved toward the scarf display. "What about her coloring? Hair, eyes, skin tone?"

"She has dark hair, getting gray now. Brown eyes. She's Filipino, so her skin is kind of olive-toned, I guess?"

"And does she like bold patterns or more subtle designs?"

"Bold, definitely. She's not shy." He smiled, relaxing slightly. "She raised four boys by herself. You kind of have to be bold for that."

"Four boys. She sounds formidable." I pulled out a few scarves, laying them across the counter. "These jewel tones would be beautiful with her coloring. The emerald green, the sapphire blue, this ruby red."

Huck examined them carefully, touching the fabrics. "These are really nice. She'd love any of them."

"The sapphire has silver threads woven through," I said, holding it up to the light. "See how it catches? That would be striking with gray hair."

"Yeah, that's perfect." He smiled genuinely for the first time. "You really know what you're doing."

"I've been at this a long time." I began wrapping the scarf in tissue paper. "How is Milo doing? He seemed stressed at the presentation yesterday."

Huck's expression darkened immediately. "He's not great, honestly. This whole thing with Lawrence is not what he expected."

"What did he expect?"

"I don't know. Partnership? Collaboration? Instead, Lawrence is treating him like an assistant. Milo does all the work and Lawrence takes all the credit." He ran a hand through his hair. "It's like Ethan all over again."

"They fought a lot, Ethan and Milo?"

"All the time. Ethan could be a real jerk sometimes, you know? He'd take Milo's designs and pass them off as his own. Promise him credit and then forget to mention him in interviews." Huck shook his head. "Milo put up with it because they were friends, but it was wearing on him."

"That must have been frustrating."

"It was killing him. And now he's in the same situation with Lawrence, except worse because at least Ethan was his friend. Lawrence is just using him." He took the wrapped package. "Thanks for this. My mom will love it."

After he left, I sat in my customer chair, thinking.

Milo suffering under Ethan's shadow. Now suffering under Lawrence's shadow. He'd traded one taskmaster for another.

Unless that was the plan all along. Unless he'd made a deal with Lawrence, and now Lawrence had changed the terms.

The rest of the afternoon was quieter. By the time I locked up at five, I was exhausted but exhilarated. Years since the shop had been this busy, since people had been this interested in my work.

As Pippa and I walked home, I turned everything over in my mind. Elise pointing at Jamie. Huck revealing Milo's continued frustrations. Lawrence's convenient takeover.

And underneath it all, Patricia's words about a runway show. About opportunity. About reminding everyone why my name mattered.

I needed to talk to Mel Tanner again. Someone who'd known Ethan well, who might know what he was planning before he died.

But first, I needed to update my notes. The picture was getting clearer, piece by piece.

Not complete yet. But closer.

Chapter Fourteen

My body woke me at five-thirty, protesting yesterday's long hours on my feet. I lay there for a moment, thinking about everything Huck had revealed. Milo trapped under Lawrence's thumb, just as he'd been trapped under Ethan's.

Unless he'd made that trap himself.

After my treadmill session and Pippa's breakfast, I opened the door to retrieve my morning newspaper.

No newspaper. Just a single piece of paper, folded in half, lying on my doormat.

My heart knew before my brain caught up. I picked it up with careful fingers, unfolded it.

Three words in block letters. Black marker.

STOP ASKING QUESTIONS!

I stepped back inside, locked the door. My hands trembled slightly as I photographed the note, then slipped it into a plastic bag.

Pippa pressed against my legs, sensing something wrong.

"Someone's getting nervous, girl."

The handwriting was deliberately disguised. All capitals, impossible to trace. Standard printer paper, nothing distinctive. Whoever left this had been careful. Professional.

Which told me more than they probably intended.

I looked at the clock. Six-thirty. Too early to call Detective Keller, though part of me knew I should. But what would I tell her? That I'd been investigating on my own and now someone wanted me to stop? She'd either shut me down or start asking questions I wasn't ready to answer.

The note was meant to scare me. Which meant I was close to something important enough that the killer felt threatened.

Good.

I dressed carefully, choosing a burnt orange wrap dress with a geometric pattern and comfortable flats. If someone was watching, I'd give them nothing to see but a harmless old lady going about her day.

"Breakfast time, Pippa. Let's go see Annie."

At the diner, I forced myself to act normal. Annie's warm greeting, Martin's grunt from his usual counter spot, eggs and toast arriving perfectly cooked. But I watched the door each time it opened, catalogued every face.

"You alright, hon?" Annie refilled my coffee, her expression concerned. "You seem jumpy."

"Didn't sleep well. Strange dreams."

"Well, you take care of yourself." She smiled at Pippa. "Both of you."

Walking to the shop, I checked reflections in windows, noted who was behind me, who turned when I turned. Old habits from my childhood, spying through the hotel's dumbwaiters. Except now the stakes were considerably higher.

Inside the shop, door locked, I finally breathed easier. I got Pippa settled in her window bed, turned on lights, arranged displays.

Then I called Mel Tanner.

"Tanner Studios."

"Dora Lee Griffen for Mel. It's urgent."

A pause, then Mel's voice. "Twice in one week. What's happened?"

"Someone left me a threatening note this morning. Told me to stop asking questions."

Silence. Then, "Maybe you should listen."

"I can't. Not when I'm this close." I kept my voice low, even though the shop was empty. "Mel, you said Lawrence had a source inside Ethan's circle. Someone feeding him information."

"Rumors only. Nothing concrete."

"Who did people suspect?"

"If I had to guess?" He paused. "Someone with complete access. Someone Ethan trusted absolutely."

"Milo."

"That would be my guess. But Dora Lee, if you're right, if they worked together, then you're dealing with people who've already committed murder."

"I know."

"Then go to the police. Let them handle it."

"Once I have proof." A customer appeared at the door, peering through the glass. "I have to go. Thank you, Mel."

"Watch your back, Dora Lee."

The morning brought a steady stream of customers. I smiled, helped, made sales. But my mind kept turning over what Mel had confirmed.

Milo and Lawrence. Partners in murder.

Except Milo seemed miserable. Trapped. Which meant either he was an excellent actor, or something had gone wrong with their plan.

Around one o'clock, my phone rang.

Viola.

"Dora Lee, have you heard?"

"Heard what?"

"About Jamie Patton. She was hit by a car this morning. Hit and run. She's in the ICU at Mount Sinai."

The shop seemed to tilt slightly. "When?"

"Around nine. She was crossing the street near her apartment and a car just plowed into her. Didn't even stop." Viola's voice carried that particular tone she used when delivering bad news. Almost relishing it. "It's her own fault for being so careless. She never looked before stepping out."

The blame. So, casual. So, quick.

"Is she going to survive?"

"They don't know yet. Critical condition. Broken bones, internal injuries." A pause. "Though between you and me, I can't help but notice the timing. First Ethan, now Jamie. Both connected to that brand."

"You think it's connected."

"Don't you?" Her voice dropped, intimate. Confidential. "Someone is tying up loose ends, Dora Lee. And you've been asking a lot of questions lately. If I were you, I'd be very careful."

There it was. The warning wrapped in concern. The threat disguised as friendship.

"I appreciate you thinking of me, Vi."

"I'm serious. Whoever did this is dangerous. They've already killed once and now they've tried again. Don't make yourself a target."

After we hung up, I stood there thinking about Viola's words. How quickly she'd moved to blame Jamie. How easily she'd connected it to Ethan's death. How smoothly she'd warned me off.

Almost like she'd been practicing.

The afternoon continued with more customers. A woman bought three dresses. A young designer wanted an interview. A vintage fashion blog wanted to feature my shop.

I smiled through it all, but my mind was elsewhere.

Jamie in the ICU. The same Jamie that both Viola and Elise had pointed to as suspicious. If she died, the case would close with her. Convenient.

Too convenient.

By five o'clock, I was exhausted. As Pippa and I walked home, I paid attention to everything. Cars, pedestrians, sounds. Someone was watching. Someone knew what I was doing.

And they'd made their position clear.

Back in my apartment, I pulled out my legal pad and wrote quickly, capturing everything before it faded.

NEW DEVELOPMENTS:

Threatening note at door: "STOP ASKING QUESTIONS!" Left sometime between midnight and 6:30am. Professional. Careful.

Mel confirmed Lawrence had inside source. Suspects Milo.

Jamie hit by car, 9am, critical condition at Mount Sinai ICU. Hit and run.

Timing: Note delivered, then Jamie attacked same morning. Coordinated?

Viola called with news. First response: blame Jamie ("her own fault"). Cold. Calculated.

Viola's warning about being careful. Genuine or threat?

Pattern: Both Viola and Elise pushed Jamie as suspect. Setting her up?

THEORY:

Milo and Lawrence worked together to eliminate Ethan.

Plan went wrong. Lawrence double-crossed Milo?

Jamie attacked to silence her or frame her posthumously.

Someone wants me to stop investigating. Desperate enough to threaten, to attack.

Question: Is Viola involved? Her behavior increasingly suspicious. Always steering, always controlling information.

I sat back, studying my notes. The pieces were there, scattered across the page like fabric swatches waiting to be sewn together.

Jamie was in the hospital now. Once she recovered, if she recovered, I needed to talk to her. Find out what she saw, what she knew.

Until then, I needed to be very, very careful.

Because whoever had left that note, whoever had tried to kill Jamie, wouldn't hesitate to come after me if I got too close to the truth.

The question was: how close was I already?

Chapter Fifteen

I'd just finished helping a customer when Elise walked in Thursday afternoon, arriving to pick up the dress she'd ordered.

"How does it look?" I asked as she emerged from the dressing room.

"Perfect. Absolutely perfect." She turned in front of the mirror, examining the fit. "You're a magician with fabric."

As I rang up her purchase, she mentioned casually, "I heard Jamie Patton got moved out of the ICU yesterday. Regular room now."

My hands stilled on the register. "She's doing better, then?"

"Still pretty banged up, but the doctors say she's going to recover. She got lucky."

Lucky. Strange word for someone who'd been deliberately run down. "Which hospital?"

"Mount Sinai. Room 412, I think." Elise studied me. "Are you going to visit her?"

"I thought I might. Bring her some flowers."

"That's nice of you." She took her bag, paused at the door. "You know, the police think it might have been an accident. That the driver panicked and fled."

"Do you believe that?"

She shrugged. "I don't know what to believe anymore. But if you visit, tell her I hope she feels better."

After Elise left, I looked at Pippa. "What do you think, girl? Time to pay Jamie a visit?"

She opened one eye, unimpressed with being woken from her nap.

I closed the shop early. Thursday afternoon, slow day, nothing that couldn't wait.

At a small flower shop near the hospital, I chose a modest arrangement. Yellow daisies and white roses in a simple glass vase. The kind of flowers that said "get well soon" without presuming intimacy.

Mount Sinai sprawled across several city blocks, all modern architecture and controlled chaos. I left Pippa at home for this. Hospitals had rules about dogs, even adorable ones.

The fourth floor was quieter than the lobby. Long hallways, hushed voices, that particular hospital smell of antiseptic and cafeteria food. I found Room 412 and knocked softly.

"Come in."

Jamie looked nothing like the beautiful model I'd met at my shop. Her face was a canvas of bruises, one eye swollen nearly shut. Her left arm rested in a cast. Bandages peeked out from under her hospital gown.

"Miss Dora Lee?" Genuine surprise. "What are you doing here?"

"I heard about your accident." I held up the flowers. "Thought you might like these."

"That's really sweet. Thank you." She gestured with her good hand. "You can put them on the windowsill."

I set the vase down, moving aside an elaborate bouquet of expensive roses. A card was attached. I glanced at it, seemingly casual.

"Get well soon. We need you back on your feet. - LJ"

Lawrence Jung. Interesting that he'd reach out to someone he barely knew. Unless he was keeping tabs on potential witnesses.

"Lots of visitors?" I settled into the chair beside her bed.

"A few. Mostly industry people sending flowers out of obligation." She shifted, winced. "The doctors say I'm lucky. Broken arm, broken ribs, concussion, lots of bruising. But nothing permanent."

"Do you remember what happened?"

Her expression clouded. "Not really. I was crossing the street, waiting for the light, and then nothing until I woke up here." She paused. "The police said it was a hit and run. Driver probably panicked."

"But you don't think so."

She looked at me for a long moment. "Miss Dora Lee, can I ask you something?"

"Of course."

"Why are you really here? We barely know each other. So, why would you visit me in the hospital?"

I could have kept playing the sweet old lady. But something about the way she looked at me, vulnerable and scared, made me choose honesty.

"Because I think someone tried to kill you. And I think it's connected to Ethan Kemper's murder."

Relief washed over her face. "I've been thinking the same thing. But the police keep saying I'm confused because of the concussion. That witnesses saw me step into traffic."

"Did you?"

"No." Her voice was firm. "I was on the sidewalk, waiting for the light. And then this car just came at me. Up onto the sidewalk. It was deliberate, Miss Dora Lee. Someone tried to kill me."

"Did you see the driver?"

"No. It happened too fast. All I remember is this dark car, maybe black or dark blue, coming right at me." She looked down at her cast. "Then nothing."

"Have you told the police?"

"I tried. I really tried, but again, they said I must be confused." She laughed bitterly, then winced. "No one believes me."

"I believe you."

Her good eye filled with tears. "Thank you. I was starting to think I was going crazy."

"You're not crazy. Someone wanted you dead, or at least badly hurt." I leaned forward slightly. "Jamie, do you know why? Did you see something? Hear something about Ethan's death?"

"I don't think so." She wiped her eyes with her good hand. "I've been trying to figure it out. Why would someone come after me?"

"Maybe because you were vocal about your anger toward Ethan. Maybe someone thought you'd make a convenient scapegoat."

"You mean frame me? Make it look like I killed Ethan and then had some kind of accident?"

"It's possible."

She was quiet, thinking. Then, "There was something. I don't know if it matters. A few weeks before Ethan died, I saw him with someone at a restaurant in SoHo. Piccolo's, on Spring Street."

My pulse quickened, but I kept my expression merely curious. "Having dinner?"

"They were arguing. I was walking by and saw them through the window. Ethan looked angry, which was unusual. He was always so controlled about everything."

"Man or woman?"

"I couldn't tell. They were sitting with their back to the window. All I could see was dark hair, average build. Could have been either." She shifted, grimacing. "I didn't think much of it at the time. But now I wonder if it's connected."

"Do you remember anything else? What they were wearing? How they moved?"

"No. It was just a glimpse through the window." She looked worried. "I might have mentioned it to someone at an audition. We were gossiping about Ethan, and I said something about him having drama in his personal life too. Do you think that's why someone came after me? Because I saw something I shouldn't have?"

"I don't know. But it's possible."

A nurse came in to check vitals, and I stood to give them space. After she left, I moved back to the chair but didn't sit down yet.

"Jamie, can I ask you something? Once you're healed, once this is all behind you, what will you do? Will you keep modeling?"

She looked surprised by the question. "I don't know. After everything that's happened, after Ethan dropping me and then this... I'm not sure anyone will want to work with me. I might have burned too many bridges."

"Nonsense. You're talented, you're resilient, and you're a survivor. That shows in your face, even now." I studied her for a moment. "When you're ready, when you're healed, come see me. I might have something for you."

"Really?"

"Really. The industry needs people with strength, not just beauty. You have both."

Fresh tears filled her eyes, but these looked different. Hopeful. "Thank you, Miss Dora Lee. That means more than you know."

"You focus on getting better. We'll talk about the rest later." I pulled out one of my shop cards and set it on her bedside table. "My number is on there. And I mean it. Call me when you're ready."

"I will. And Miss Dora Lee? Thank you. For believing me. For caring enough to come here."

"Of course. You just focus on getting better."

I stepped into the hallway and nearly collided with Milo Savage.

"Miss Dora Lee." Surprise flickered across his face. "What are you doing here?"

"Visiting Jamie. Bringing flowers." I kept my tone pleasant. "What brings you here?"

"Same thing. Checking on her." He held up a small teddy bear from the gift shop. "I heard about the accident."

Both Milo and Lawrence reaching out to Jamie. Concerned friends? Or making sure she stayed quiet?

"That's kind of you."

We stood there, the moment stretching awkwardly. Then Milo looked past me into Jamie's room.

"Is she doing okay?"

"Recovering. She's stronger than she looks."

He nodded but didn't move to go in. "Miss Dora Lee, can I ask you something?"

"Of course."

"That night I came to your apartment. When I was drunk and rambling." He ran a hand through his hair. "Did I say anything I shouldn't have?"

"Like what?"

"I don't know. I was pretty out of it. I've been trying to remember." His eyes were dark, worried. "I've been making a lot of mistakes lately. Trusting the wrong people. Saying things I shouldn't say."

"You told me you loved Ethan like a brother. That you didn't kill him."

"Did you believe me?"

I studied him carefully. Exhausted. Haunted. Nothing like the angry young man in the elevator or the sullen figure beside Lawrence at the presentation.

"I don't know what I believe anymore, Milo. But I know you're in over your head with something. Whatever you're involved in, whoever you're working with, you need to be very careful."

His eyes widened slightly. "What makes you think I'm working with someone?"

"Because things don't add up. Because you're miserable even though you got what you supposedly wanted." I paused. "Because someone is trying very hard to tie up loose ends, and I'm worried you might be next."

"I didn't kill Ethan." His voice was quiet, intense. "No matter what anyone thinks, no matter how it looks, I didn't kill my best friend."

"Then who did?"

He looked at me for a long moment. I thought he might actually tell me. But then he shook his head.

"I need to go see Jamie. Make sure she's okay."

He moved past me into the room. I heard him greet Jamie warmly.

I stood in the hallway, processing. Milo was scared. Hiding something.

But was he hiding that he was a murderer? Or that he'd made a deal with one?

I pulled out my phone as I walked to the elevator, texted Mel Tanner.

"Do you know if Ethan frequented a restaurant called Piccolo's on Spring Street?"

The response came within minutes.

"Yes. His favorite. Had a regular table there. Why?"

"Just following a lead. Thank you."

I had my next destination.

Time to see what secrets Piccolo's might hold.

Chapter Sixteen

The hospital visit had eaten most of the afternoon. By the time I left Jamie's room, the sun had started its descent, casting long shadows across the city streets.

I was exhausted. The kind of bone-deep tired that reminded me I was seventy-eight years old and had, in the past week, climbed through a dumbwaiter shaft, attended a high-profile fashion presentation, and spent hours at Mount Sinai visiting an injured woman. My back ached from the dumbwaiter adventure. My legs felt heavy. Even my hands hurt from gripping the old ropes.

But I still needed to eat. The hospital breakfast seemed like days ago.

I spotted Carlo's Market on the corner, a small neighborhood bodega I'd passed countless times on my way to and from the Royal Griffen. Carlo had run it for almost thirty years, and before that, his father had owned it. I'd watched the place change hands, watched Carlo grow from a young man helping his father to the weathered shopkeeper he was now.

The bell chimed as I pushed open the door. The market was narrow, crammed with shelves of canned goods, fresh produce in wooden crates, a small refrigerated section in back. It smelled like coffee and fresh bread and something vaguely spicy I couldn't quite identify.

"Miss Dora Lee!" Carlo looked up from behind the counter, his weathered face breaking into a warm smile. "I haven't seen you in weeks. You feeling okay?"

"Just tired, Carlo. Long day."

"Ah, I heard about the trouble at your building. That young designer." He shook his head sadly. "Terrible thing. You knew him?"

"A little. Just as a neighbor."

"Still." He came around the counter, moving with the ease of someone who'd walked these same aisles for decades. "What can I get for you tonight? Something easy, yes? You look worn out."

"Some soup, maybe some bread."

"I have fresh tomato basil. Maria made it this morning." He pulled a container from the refrigerated sixtion. "And bread, of course. Still warm from this afternoon."

I followed him through the narrow aisles, my feet protesting every step. He selected a small round loaf wrapped in paper and handed it to me with care.

"This one's the best. The crust, just right."

As I made my way to grab some milk, I felt it. That prickling sensation on the back of my neck. The awareness of being watched.

I turned, scanning the store. Just Carlo restocking a shelf near the front, and an elderly woman examining vegetables by the window. No one else.

I shook it off and grabbed the milk, adding a small container of butter.

But the feeling persisted. Stronger now.

I moved back toward the counter, my eyes darting to the windows. People passed on the sidewalk outside, but none of them looked in. None of them seemed to notice me.

"You sure you're okay?" Carlo was watching me with concern as he rang up my items. "You keep looking around like you lost something."

"I'm fine. Just jumpy, I guess."

"These are difficult times." He placed my items in a brown paper bag with careful hands. "Police cars at your building, people talking. Makes everyone nervous." He met my eyes. "You lock your doors, yes? An old building like that, lots of ways in and out."

"I do. Thank you, Carlo."

"Maria worries about you up there alone. She says to me, 'Carlo, Miss Dora Lee needs to eat more.' So, next time, you take some of her minestrone. I'll save you some."

"That's very kind."

I paid and took the bag, heavier than I'd expected. My arms would feel this tomorrow.

Outside, the feeling intensified. I paused on the sidewalk, looking left and right. A woman with a stroller. A man in a business suit walking quickly past. A teenager on a skateboard.

Normal city life.

But someone was watching. I could feel it.

I started walking toward the Royal Griffen, my pace slower than usual. Every few steps, I glanced over my shoulder. Nothing. No one following. No one paying attention to me at all.

Just an old woman carrying groceries home.

But my heart raced anyway. My hands gripped the paper bag tighter.

By the time I reached the Royal Griffen, my exhaustion had compounded. The bag felt like it weighed fifty pounds. My shoulders ached. My feet screamed for rest.

The lobby hummed with late-day activity. And there, near the front desk talking to Chelsea and Melanie, stood Detective Keller.

All three women looked serious. Focused.

Walter greeted me at the door with his usual smile. "Afternoon, Miss Dora Lee. Good day?"

"Just fine, Walter. Thank you."

I shuffled toward the elevator, the grocery bag weighing down one arm, moving slowly enough to listen.

"So, you finished the search?" Chelsea was asking.

"Yes, we executed the warrant this afternoon while Mr. Savage was out." Detective Keller's voice carried that official tone. "Toxicology came back. Ethan Kemper had amphetamines in his system when he died."

My shuffling slowed even more.

"Amphetamines?" Melanie's voice rose. "Like drugs?"

"Could be prescription, could be recreational. The levels were high enough that combined with the heat of the sauna, it likely caused cardiac arrest." Detective Keller paused. "We searched the apartment looking for the source. Prescription bottles, stash, anything. Came up empty."

"So, he didn't take them himself?" Chelsea asked.

"We don't know. He could have gotten them elsewhere, taken them before coming to the gym. Or someone could have given them to him without his knowledge."

"You mean someone drugged him?" Melanie sounded horrified.

"It's a possibility we're investigating. Have either of you noticed anything unusual lately? Anyone hanging around who shouldn't be?"

Chelsea thought for a moment. "We did have someone try to access the service entrance. Jerry caught them and sent them away."

"When was this?"

"Last Thursday. Around three in the afternoon. Jerry logged it."

Last Thursday. The day after Ethan died.

Detective Keller made a note. "Description?"

"Delivery uniform. Baseball cap, sunglasses. Jerry said they claimed to have the wrong address, but he didn't buy it."

"I'll need to speak with Jerry."

I reached the elevator and pressed the button, shifting the grocery bag to my other arm. My shoulders protested the movement.

"Oh, and Detective?" Melanie's voice dropped slightly. "That lady came by again. The one who's been asking about Miss Dora Lee."

My finger froze over the button.

"Hold the elevator?"

Milo Savage.

The doors had opened without me noticing. I held them, my heart rate kicking up as he stepped in beside me. Behind us, I could hear Melanie still talking to Detective Keller, but Milo pressed five and the doors began to slide shut.

"...described her as older, well dressed, very persistent about..."

The doors closed, cutting off the rest.

I stood there, the grocery bag clutched against my chest, my mind spinning. Someone asking about me. Older. Well dressed. Persistent.

But I couldn't think about that now. Not with Milo standing inches away.

The elevator began its slow ascent.

Silence filled the small space. Milo stood perfectly still, staring straight ahead. I could feel the tension radiating off him.

I kept my eyes on the floor numbers lighting up above the door. One. Two. Three.

The elevator creaked and groaned, its old mechanisms protesting.

Four.

Milo shifted slightly.

The elevator approached five.

Milo shifted again. I could feel him looking at me. When I glanced over, I saw his reflection in the polished elevator doors. His jaw was working, clenching and unclenching. His hands were shaking.

The elevator dinged and slid open on five.

He didn't move at first. Just stood there, breathing too fast, too shallow. Like someone on the edge of panic. Then he turned to face me, and I saw his eyes.

They weren't cold. They were terrified.

"I'm on to you."

His voice cracked on the last word. Not threatening. Desperate. Like a cornered animal that knows it has nowhere left to run. His hands clenched into fists at his sides, then opened again, trembling visibly.

"I know what you're doing," he continued, his voice barely above a whisper. "The questions. The investigating. You're going to ruin everything."

I opened my mouth to respond, but he was already stepping backward into the hallway, his chest rising and falling rapidly. He looked like he might be sick. Or cry. Or both.

He stood there as the doors began to close, and I saw the sheen of sweat on his forehead despite the cool elevator. His eyes stayed locked on mine, wide and panicked.

Not the eyes of someone threatening me.

The eyes of someone drowning.

The doors slid shut, cutting off his stare.

The elevator lurched upward. I stood there, my heart pounding, my hands trembling so badly the grocery bag rustled.

I'm on to you.

Not a threat. A plea.

He wasn't warning me to stop investigating.

He was begging me to.

What did he know? How much had he figured out? And more importantly, what was he so afraid I would discover?

Or had I already discovered it, and he knew his time was running out?

The doors opened on ten. I stepped out on shaking legs, the grocery bag bumping against my hip as I hurried down the hallway to my apartment.

Inside, Pippa greeted me enthusiastically, but I barely registered her welcome. I set the groceries on the counter with trembling hands, locked the door, put the chain on, then leaned against it, trying to catch my breath.

Milo knew. He knew I was investigating. Knew I'd been asking questions, digging into things.

Did he know about the photos? About the evidence I'd found in his apartment that night through the dumbwaiter?

I moved to the window, looking down at the street below. People going about their normal lives, oblivious to the fact that a murderer lived in this building.

And that murderer had just threatened me.

Because that's what it was. A threat. "I'm on to you" wasn't a friendly observation. It was a warning.

I fed Pippa with shaking hands, then made myself soup I couldn't eat. The soup Carlo had recommended sat on the counter. The aroma filled the air, but it just caused my stomach to churn instead of soothe me.

My mind kept replaying that moment in the elevator. The way he'd turned. The flatness in his voice. The coldness in his eyes.

That feeling of being watched at Carlo's Market. Had that been him? Had Milo been following me?

Finally, I pulled out my legal pad and forced myself to write. NEW DEVELOPMENTS:

TOXICOLOGY: Amphetamines found in Ethan's system. High levels. Combined with sauna heat = cardiac arrest.

Police searched apartment today (while I was at hospital visiting Jamie). Found nothing. No prescription bottles, no drug source.

Questions: Did Ethan take them willingly? Or was he drugged without knowledge?

If drugged, who had access? Milo lived with him. Easy to slip into food/drink.

Jamie confirmed deliberate attack, dark car onto sidewalk

Saw Ethan arguing with someone at Piccolo's weeks before death, dark hair, average build, gender unclear

Jamie mentioned this at audition, possible reason for attack

Both Milo and Lawrence reached out to Jamie in hospital (keeping tabs?)

Someone tried service entrance day after murder, delivery uniform, baseball cap, sunglasses, unidentified

Someone looking for me at building (per Melanie), older, well dressed, persistent, who?

My hands still shaking slightly as I added new observations:

MILO CONFRONTATION IN ELEVATOR: "I'm on to you"

Not angry. Scared. Terrified, actually.

Physical signs: hands shaking, jaw clenching, breathing fast and shallow, sweating despite cool temperature, eyes wide and panicked.

Voice cracked when he spoke. Desperate, not threatening.

"You're going to ruin everything." What does he think I'm going to ruin? His partnership with Lawrence? Or something much worse?

He looked like someone drowning. Like someone who knows the truth is about to come out and there's nothing he can do to stop it.

Question: Does he know I broke into the apartment? Does he know about the photos?

Or is he just afraid because he knows I'm smart enough to figure it out eventually?

Either way, he's unraveling. Fast.

THEORY:

Milo drugged Ethan with amphetamines, lured him to sauna

Heat + drugs = heart attack

Lawrence involved? Possibly planned together

Jamie targeted to silence or frame

Person at Piccolo's is key

Milo now KNOWS I'm investigating = I'm in danger

I sat back, staring at my notes. The amphetamines changed everything. This wasn't just locking someone in a sauna and hoping they overheated. This was premeditated. Calculated. Someone had drugged Ethan specifically to ensure the sauna would kill him.

And Milo, who lived with Ethan, had the easiest access.

But now Milo knew I was onto him. Which made me a target.

I looked around my apartment. The chair under the doorknob suddenly seemed inadequate. The chain on the door felt flimsy.

Tomorrow, I would go to Piccolo's. Find out who Ethan had been arguing with. Get answers.

But tonight, I needed to survive.

I double-checked every lock. Pushed the chair more firmly under the doorknob. Even wedged a heavy book against the chair for extra security.

Pippa watched my frantic preparations with worried eyes.

"It's okay, girl. We're okay."

But I wasn't sure I believed it.

I lay in bed, fully dressed, my phone on the nightstand with Detective Keller's number pulled up and ready to dial.

Every sound made me jump. Every creak of the building sent my heart racing.

And five floors below me, Milo Savage knew I was investigating him.

The question was: what would he do about it?

Chapter Seventeen

I barely slept that night. Every sound in the building had me on edge. The radiator hissing. Footsteps in the hallway outside my door. The elevator creaking as it moved between floors far below.

Around three in the morning, I gave up entirely. I walked through my apartment checking every lock for the third time, testing the chain on the door, making sure the chair was wedged firmly under the doorknob. My hands shook as I did it.

Pippa followed me from room to room, her ears drooping with concern. She knew something was wrong.

"It's okay, girl," I whispered, but my voice cracked on the words.

I made chamomile tea and sat at my kitchen table, wrapping both hands around the warm mug. Pippa pressed against my legs, offering what comfort she could.

"This is ridiculous," I told her. "I've lived in this building my entire life. I'm not going to let some murderer scare me out of my own home."

She yawned, unconvinced.

But my body was convinced. My shoulders ached from tension. My back hurt from the dumbwaiter climb two nights ago. My feet were sore from all the walking yesterday. And my chest felt tight with fear that wouldn't quite loosen its grip.

I was seventy-eight years old, and I felt every single year of it.

By the time morning came, I was exhausted but grimly determined. Today I would go to Piccolo's and find out who Ethan had been arguing with. That person could be the key to everything.

After my usual treadmill routine, which I cut short because my legs protested every step, I dressed in comfortable clothes. Wide-leg pants in soft gray, a loose tunic in shades of blue and green, and flat shoes that wouldn't punish my aching feet. I added a long scarf for color, but when I looked in the mirror, I could see the exhaustion in my face. Dark circles under my eyes. Lines that seemed deeper than yesterday.

"Come on, Pippa. Let's get some breakfast."

The diner was busier than usual for a Friday morning. Martin was at his usual spot at the counter. He glanced at me as I came in, then did a double take.

"You look terrible," he said bluntly.

"Good morning to you too, Martin."

"I'm serious. You sick?"

"Just didn't sleep well."

Annie appeared with coffee and her usual warm smile, but her expression shifted to concern when she got a good look at me. "Oh honey, you okay? You look worn out."

"Long week."

"You sit right down. I'll get you the usual, and I'm adding extra bacon for Miss Pippa. You both need some comfort food." She poured my coffee, then touched my shoulder gently. "Whatever's going on, it'll work out. You hear me?"

"I hear you."

But as I sat in our usual booth, my coffee untouched in front of me, I wasn't so sure. My mind kept replaying the elevator scene. Milo's flat voice. His cold eyes. "I'm on to you."

He knew I was investigating. Which meant I was in danger. Real danger.

Pippa put her paws on the seat beside me, whining softly.

"I know, girl. I'm scared too."

Annie brought our food, but I barely tasted it. My mind was elsewhere, turning over everything I knew, trying to see the pattern I kept missing.

When we finally made it to the shop, my feet were dragging. I unlocked the door and turned on the lights, the familiar routine usually comforting but today feeling mechanical. Empty.

Pippa settled into her window bed without her usual three turns and digging routine. She just curled up and watched me with worried eyes.

The morning passed in a blur of customers. Four people came in. Three bought things. I smiled and chatted and wrapped purchases, but part of me stayed alert, watching the door, wondering if Milo might walk in. Wondering if I was being watched even now.

Around one o'clock, during a lull, I made a decision. I was going to Piccolo's. I was going to find out who that person was. I was going to solve this, no matter how scared I felt.

"Come on, Pippa. We're going out for lunch today."

The taxi dropped us off on Spring Street in SoHo. Piccolo's was exactly the kind of place I'd expected, a charming Italian restaurant with a green awning and small tables visible through large windows. The kind of intimate spot where fashion industry people would go for business meetings.

I pushed open the door. The smell of garlic and fresh bread enveloped me immediately, making my stomach growl despite my nerves.

A hostess in a crisp white shirt smiled at me. "Good afternoon. Table for one?"

"Yes, please. Somewhere quiet if you have it."

"Of course. Right this way."

She led me to a small table near the window. Not quite in the corner, but positioned so I could see most of the restaurant. It was about half full, mostly well-dressed professionals lingering over lunch. Exposed brick walls, warm lighting, framed photos of the Italian countryside. Cozy. Inviting.

I should have felt relaxed. Instead, my shoulders stayed tense, my back rigid in the chair.

Pippa settled under the table with a soft sigh. Even she seemed tired.

"Your server will be right with you."

I looked over the menu, the words swimming slightly. When was the last time I'd slept properly? Two days ago? Three?

A young waiter appeared with water and bread. "Can I start you with something to drink?"

"Just water is fine, thank you."

"Have you been here before?"

"First time, actually. A friend of mine recommended it. Ethan Kemper. He said this place had the best Italian food in SoHo." I kept my tone light, casual, even though my heart was beating faster.

The waiter's expression shifted immediately, becoming sad. "Mr. Kemper. Yes, he was a regular. Such a tragedy what happened to him."

"Did you know him well?"

"A bit. I waited on him many times. Always very polite, good tipper." He gestured to the corner table. "That was his favorite spot."

"He had good taste in restaurants, that's for sure. I'm sorry I waited so long to try it."

"Well, let me make sure your first visit is memorable. Can I recommend the osso buco? It was Mr. Kemper's favorite."

"That sounds perfect."

He took my order and disappeared into the kitchen. A few minutes later, an older man emerged. I recognized him immediately as the owner type, the way he moved through the dining room with easy confidence, checking on tables, nodding to regulars.

He noticed me looking at the corner table and came over.

"I couldn't help but overhear that you knew Ethan," he said with a kind smile. "I'm Marco Benedetti. I own Piccolo's."

"Dora Lee Griffen. Nice to meet you."

"Ah, you're the one who ordered the osso buco. An excellent choice." He gestured to the chair across from me. "May I sit for a moment?"

"Of course."

He settled into the chair with a contented sigh, like someone who'd been on his feet all morning. "Ethan was a good customer. A good man. We were all very sad to hear what happened." He shook his head. "How did you know him?"

"We lived in the same building. The Royal Griffen. I didn't know him well, but he seemed like a sweet young man. He mentioned this restaurant several times, said it was his favorite place in the city."

"That's very kind of him to say." Marco looked genuinely touched. "He came here often. At least once a week, sometimes more."

"Did he usually come alone?"

"Sometimes. Other times he brought friends, business associates. Fashion people, you know. They all come here." He said it with a mix of pride and resignation. "In fact, I'm just now realizing, you're Dora Lee Griffen, the fashion designer. My wife loves your work!"

"That's very sweet."

"She has one of your pieces from the nineties, a dress with these beautiful colors. She says it's her favorite thing she owns."

"I'm so glad she enjoys it."

The waiter brought my osso buco. The meat was falling off the bone, and the aroma made my mouth water despite my exhaustion.

"Please, enjoy your lunch. But if you don't mind me asking, you said you lived in the same building where Ethan died?"

"Yes. It's been quite unsettling, actually. The police have been investigating, trying to understand what happened."

Marco leaned forward slightly, lowering his voice. "Can I tell you something? Something that's been bothering me?"

My pulse quickened. "Of course."

"A few weeks before Ethan died, maybe three weeks, he came in late one night. Around nine o'clock. He was meeting someone here, and their conversation seemed very tense."

I took a bite of the osso buco, forcing myself to chew slowly, to look only mildly curious even though my heart was pounding. "Oh?"

"It was a woman. I didn't get a good look at her face because she was wearing large sunglasses. At night. Inside the restaurant." He shook his head. "Very strange."

"That is odd. Could you tell anything else about her?"

"Tall, maybe five-eight or five-nine. Slender. Dark hair, shoulder length. Well dressed, expensive clothes. She had that polished look, you know? Expensive taste, sophisticated."

I took another bite, my mind already racing through possibilities. "Did you hear what they were talking about?"

"Not most of it. But at one point, Ethan raised his voice enough that I heard him say something like, 'You promised me.' The woman, she kept looking around, like she didn't want anyone to see her. Then she left in a hurry, practically ran out the door. Ethan stayed for a while longer, looking very upset."

"Have you told the police about this?"

"No one asked. They came by asking about Ethan, but they wanted to know about his regular habits, who he usually came with. They didn't ask about that specific night." He paused. "Do you think it's important?"

"It might be. Detective Keller is handling the case. You should give her a call."

"I will." He stood up. "I should let you enjoy your meal."

He started to walk away, then turned back. "Oh, one more thing. Are you going to the Valentina Rossi show tomorrow night?"

"The Valentina Rossi show?"

"She's this young designer, very hot right now. Having a big show at the Bowery Hotel tomorrow evening. All the fashion people are talking about it." He smiled. "My wife is catering the after-party, that's how I know. She said half the industry will be there."

A fashion show where half the industry would be present. That meant suspects, potential witnesses, people who might know something.

"I hadn't heard about it. Is it invitation only?"

"Usually, but my wife might be able to get you in. She'd be thrilled to help, especially since you're Dora Lee Griffen. Let me call her." He pulled out his phone and stepped away, speaking rapidly in Italian.

I sat there, my fork suspended halfway to my mouth, my mind working through Marco's description.

A tall, slender woman with dark hair. Wearing sunglasses at night inside the restaurant, clearly trying to hide her identity. Meeting with Ethan three weeks before his death. Arguing with him. And Ethan had said, "You promised me."

The description could fit several people. Jamie had red hair, not dark. Ellie was blonde. Elise had dark hair and was tall, but would she have reason to meet secretly with Ethan?

Or could it have been Viola?

The thought hit me like a physical blow. My fork clattered onto my plate.

Viola was tall. Slender. She had platinum blonde hair now, but she'd had dark hair for most of her life. I'd known her for over forty years. I could picture her exactly as Marco described. Polished. Sophisticated. Expensive taste. She fit perfectly.

And she could have been wearing a wig.

My stomach clenched. No. No, not Viola. Not my oldest friend.

But the pieces started clicking together with horrible clarity. I thought about how Viola would react if I mentioned this woman to her. Would she ask pointed questions? Would she seem nervous? I could picture it perfectly, and that scared me.

She'd been steering my investigation from the very beginning. Pushing me toward Jamie. Warning me away from Lawrence. Always there with advice, with suggestions about who to suspect.

Like a chess player moving pieces on a board.

I set my fork down carefully, my hands trembling. I pressed them flat against the table, trying to steady myself.

Forty years. We'd been friends for over forty years. Through marriages and divorces and career highs and lows. She'd been at my father's funeral. I'd been at her husband's.

But what if I didn't really know her? What if the Viola I thought I knew was just the face she chose to show me?

I thought back through every conversation we'd had since Ethan's death. The way she'd immediately suggested Milo as the obvious suspect. The way she'd talked about Jamie's bitterness, her instability, her public meltdowns. The way she'd warned me to stop investigating, but in a way that almost dared me to continue.

She'd been playing me. Testing me. Watching to see how close I'd get to the truth.

But why? What could Viola have promised Ethan? What connection did they have?

I forced myself to pick up my fork again, to take another bite, to look normal even though my world had just tilted on its axis. I couldn't let Marco see that anything was wrong.

But inside, everything was wrong.

If Viola had met secretly with Ethan three weeks before his death, if they'd argued about a broken promise, then she was involved somehow. Maybe not the killer, but involved.

And I'd been confiding in her. Telling her everything I'd discovered. Asking her advice.

I'd been showing my cards to someone who might be my opponent.

The thought made me feel sick. Stupid. Naive.

But no. I wasn't naive. I was a chess player too. And chess players didn't always show their hand.

Maybe Viola didn't know how much I suspected. Maybe she thought I still trusted her completely.

And if that was true, maybe I could use that.

I took a breath, steadying myself. I needed to think this through carefully. I needed proof, not just suspicions. I couldn't accuse my oldest friend of murder conspiracy based on a vague description and some redirected conversations.

But I also couldn't ignore what I'd learned.

Marco returned, smiling. "You're in luck. My wife says she can add you to the list. Just tell them at the door you're Isabella Benedetti's guest."

"Thank you so much. That's incredibly generous."

"It's nothing. Isabella is excited to meet you tomorrow." He gestured to my plate. "Now I'll let you finish that osso buco. It's the best in SoHo."

I finished my meal mechanically, barely tasting the food that had smelled so delicious minutes ago. Marco refused to let me pay.

"Please, you're a friend of Ethan's. And tomorrow you'll tell everyone at the fashion show about Piccolo's, yes?"

"Absolutely." I pulled out one of my shop cards and pressed it into his hand. "And please, have your wife come by my shop. I'd love to meet her. I'll give her a very nice discount on anything she likes. It's the least I can do for all your kindness."

Marco's weathered face broke into a genuine smile. "She will be thrilled. Truly. Thank you, Miss Dora Lee."

"Thank you, Marco. For the wonderful meal and for the information."

"You are so welcome. Please, please come again."

Outside, I stood on the sidewalk for a moment, Pippa sitting patiently at my feet. The afternoon sun felt too bright. The street noise was too loud. Everything felt wrong.

A woman with dark hair. Wearing sunglasses at night. Arguing with Ethan about a broken promise.

It could be Viola.

Or it could be someone else entirely. Someone I hadn't even considered yet.

I hailed a taxi, my mind still churning. As we drove back uptown, I stared out the window without really seeing anything.

The letter signed "L." The maintenance keycard in Milo's gym bag. Lawrence's convenient takeover of the brand. Viola's constant redirection of suspicion. Jamie's hit and run. The mysterious woman at Piccolo's.

And underneath it all, the question I couldn't quite answer: what had someone promised Ethan? What was important enough to meet secretly, to wear a disguise, to argue about?

By the time we reached the Royal Griffen, I still didn't have answers. But I had more questions than ever.

And tomorrow night at the fashion show, I'd be surrounded by suspects. Lawrence. Milo. Possibly Viola.

One of them might be a killer.

And after Milo's threat yesterday, they all knew I was investigating.

Going to that fashion show was a risk. Maybe even dangerous.

But I was going anyway.

Because somewhere in all these pieces, there was a pattern. A truth. And I was going to find it.

Even if it meant discovering that my oldest friend had been lying to me for forty years.

Chapter Eighteen

The next day, I spent the morning at the shop, but my mind was already on the evening ahead. The Valentina Rossi show at the Bowery Hotel. Half the fashion industry would be there, including, I hoped, some answers.

And possibly a killer.

I closed the shop at three, my body protesting every movement. Another night of fractured sleep. Another day of fear sitting like a stone in my chest. I was running on fumes and determination, and I wasn't sure how much longer I could keep going.

But tonight, I needed to be someone else. Not the exhausted, frightened old woman I'd become over the past two weeks. Tonight, I needed to be Dora Lee Griffen, legendary fashion designer. Confident. Powerful. Untouchable.

Even if it was all performance.

Back at the apartment, I stood in front of my closet, considering my options. I needed armor. Something that would command respect, remind people who I was, but also allow me to blend in enough to observe without being constantly noticed.

Finally, I pulled out a piece I'd been saving for a special occasion. A floor-length gown in deep midnight blue silk with an asymmetrical neckline and subtle beading that caught the light when I moved. I'd made it two years ago but had never found the right moment to wear it.

Tonight was the moment. Tonight, I would dress like I belonged in this world. A world I once belonged to but now felt like an imposter in.

I paired it with silver heels, low enough that my aching feet could manage them but elegant enough to complete the look. A vintage silver clutch. My good jewelry: real pearls at my neck, diamond earrings that had been my mother's, and a statement cocktail ring with a sapphire that matched the dress.

My hair, which I usually wore simply, I swept up into an elegant chignon. My hands shook slightly as I pinned it, but I forced them steady.

Makeup next. More than I usually wore, but appropriate for an evening event. I studied my reflection as I applied it. The dark circles under my eyes, the lines that seemed deeper than they'd been two weeks ago. The exhaustion that makeup couldn't quite hide.

Red lipstick last. A color I rarely used but that made me feel powerful. Dangerous, even.

When I looked in the mirror, I barely recognized myself. I looked like the Dora Lee Griffen from the height of my career. Confident. Sophisticated. Ready to take on the world.

But inside, I was terrified.

"Now for you, Miss Pippa."

Pippa had been watching me get ready with interest, her tail wagging occasionally. She knew something exciting was happening.

I pulled out a special outfit I'd made for her months ago but hadn't had occasion to use. A tiny dress in silver fabric that coordinated with my gown, with a collar made of rhinestones that sparkled like real diamonds. I'd even made her a small silver bow that attached to her collar.

"You're going to be the most fashionable dog at the show," I told her as I got her dressed.

She stood patiently, used to wearing outfits, then did a little spin when I finished. She knew she looked good.

At least one of us did.

I called for a car, and when it arrived at six-thirty, the driver did a double-take when I got in.

"Wow, you look amazing! Big event tonight?"

"Fashion show at the Bowery Hotel."

"Nice. You're a designer?"

"I am."

"Cool. I bet you'll be the best dressed one there."

I smiled, though it felt like my face might crack from the effort. If only he knew that most of the people at this show would be dressed by designers far more famous and current than me. If only he knew I was walking into a room full of suspects, at least one of whom had already threatened me.

But it was a nice compliment nonetheless.

The Bowery Hotel was lit up like a jewel when we arrived. A red carpet led to the entrance, lined with photographers and fashion press. Beautiful people in incredible outfits streamed inside, the whole scene buzzing with energy and excitement.

Young energy. I suddenly felt every one of my seventy-eight years.

I took a deep breath, my ribs protesting. My chest felt tight. "Ready, Pippa?"

She wagged her tail, oblivious to my fear.

We made our way to the entrance, where a young woman with a clipboard was checking names. I moved carefully, aware that my elegant appearance was just a facade. Underneath, I was fragile. Breakable.

"Name please?"

"Dora Lee Griffen. I'm a guest of Isabella Benedetti."

She scanned her list, then her eyes widened. "The Dora Lee Griffen?"

"That would be me."

"Oh my God. This is such an honor. Please, go right in." She gestured to someone nearby. "Can someone show Miss Griffen to the VIP section?"

"That's not necessary, I can find my way."

"No, no, I insist. Valentina would kill me if I didn't take care of you properly."

A young man in all black appeared and offered his arm. "Right this way, Miss Griffen."

As we walked through the lobby, heads turned. I heard whispers.

"Is that Dora Lee Griffen?"

"I thought she'd retired."

"She looks incredible."

"That dress is stunning."

"Oh my God, her dog is wearing a matching outfit!"

I kept my chin up, my shoulders back, my face arranged in a pleasant smile. Performance. All of it performance.

Pippa, as always, loved the attention. She walked with her head high, tail wagging, giving people her most charming look.

The show was being held in the hotel's grand ballroom, which had been transformed into a runway space. Rows of chairs lined both sides of a long white runway, with standing room in the back. Dramatic lighting, pounding music, an energy that was almost electric.

The young man led me to the third row, right in the center. Prime seating.

"Is this okay? Valentina wanted to make sure you had a good view."

"This is perfect. Thank you."

"Can I get you anything? Champagne? Water?"

"Champagne would be lovely." Maybe it would steady my nerves.

He disappeared, and I settled into my seat carefully, my body grateful to rest. Pippa curled at my feet with a small sigh. Around me, the fashion elite were finding their places. Editors from major magazines, buyers from department stores, influencers with their phones already out taking photos, other designers sizing up the competition.

And there, several rows ahead, I spotted Lawrence Jung. He was talking animatedly with a group of people, holding court as usual. Next to him, looking uncomfortable in an expensive suit, was Milo.

I studied him more carefully this time, using the crowd as cover. The expensive suit hung differently than it should have. Not quite right on his frame. Had he lost weight? His face looked thinner, more drawn than when I'd seen him at the crime scene. Dark circles under his eyes suggested sleep wasn't coming easily. One hand kept going to his collar, adjusting it, a nervous gesture I recognized from my years working with anxious models.

He looked like someone carrying something heavy. Something that weighed on him every waking moment.

My heart stuttered in my chest. Both of them here, together.

Milo, who'd cornered me in the elevator. "I'm on to you."

Lawrence, who'd swooped in to take over Ethan's brand with suspicious speed.

The young man returned with my champagne. My hand trembled slightly as I took it, and I had to use both hands to raise it to my lips.

I continued scanning the crowd, my eyes moving systematically, cataloging threats.

There was Elise Golding, the model who'd told me about Jamie's meltdown. She was sitting in the second row, looking stunning in a metallic dress.

And there, near the back, was Mel Tanner, his silver hair unmistakable even in the crowded room. He saw me and raised his glass in a salute. I nodded back, grateful for one friendly face.

But I didn't see Viola. Strange. She never missed major fashion events.

"Dora Lee Griffen. I heard you were here, but I didn't believe it."

I turned to find a woman about my age settling into the seat next to me. It took me a moment to place her.

"Caroline Esper. Fashion Week 1989."

"Good memory." She laughed, but her eyes were serious. "I heard you've been making waves lately. Showing up at presentations, asking questions about that poor Kemper boy."

"Word travels fast."

"It always does in this industry." She leaned in, her voice dropping. "Be careful, Dora Lee. People are talking. And not everyone is happy about you poking around."

My fingers tightened around my champagne glass. "What people?"

"Just people. The kind who don't like their dirty laundry aired." She patted my hand, and I had to force myself not to flinch. "I'm just saying, watch your back."

Before I could ask what she meant, the lights dimmed. The music changed, becoming louder, more intense. A voice came over the sound system.

"Ladies and gentlemen, welcome to the Valentina Rossi Spring Collection show."

The crowd erupted in applause. The first model appeared at the top of the runway, and the show began.

I tried to focus on the clothes, which were actually quite good. Valentina had talent. Bold colors, interesting silhouettes, a fresh take on classic shapes. But my mind kept wandering to the people around me.

Lawrence and Milo, sitting together but not talking. Lawrence seemed relaxed, confident. Milo looked like he wanted to be anywhere else. Like he was trapped.

Elise, in the second row, taking photos of every look. Professional, focused.

Mel Tanner, watching the show with the critical eye of someone who'd seen thousands of collections.

And the mysterious absence of Viola. Where was she?

Unless she was avoiding me. Unless she knew I'd been to Piccolo's, knew what Marco might have told me.

Halfway through the show, during a quick transition, I felt my phone buzz in my clutch. I pulled it out discreetly.

A text from an unknown number:

"You should leave. Now."

The champagne glass nearly slipped from my fingers. I set it down carefully on the floor beneath my chair, my hands shaking too badly to hold it.

I looked around, trying to see who might have sent it. But everyone was focused on the runway. Anonymous faces in the dark.

Another buzz.

"I'm warning you for your own good. Leave before something happens."

My throat constricted. I couldn't breathe properly. The corset bodice of my dress suddenly felt too tight, crushing my ribs.

Someone here knew I was investigating. Someone was watching me right now. In this very room.

And they wanted me gone.

I forced myself to take slow breaths. To keep my face neutral. To stay in my seat even though every instinct screamed at me to run.

But I wasn't leaving. Not when I was this close.

The show continued. Models walked. The audience applauded. And I sat there, my body rigid with fear, my mind racing through possibilities.

Who had my number? Who knew I'd be here?

As the final model walked and Valentina came out for her bow, the crowd stood and cheered. I stood too, my legs unsteady beneath me. Pippa pressed against my legs, whining softly. She could sense something was wrong.

"Beautiful show," Caroline said beside me. "Are you going to the after-party?"

My voice came out steadier than I felt. "I wasn't planning on it."

"You should. Everyone will be there. It might be interesting." The way she said "interesting" made me think she knew something. Or was warning me.

The crowd started moving toward the exits, where the after-party would be held in another part of the hotel. I joined the flow of people, keeping Pippa close, my eyes scanning constantly for threats.

In the hallway, I was stopped multiple times by people wanting to say hello, compliment my dress, ask about my shop. I smiled and chatted, my face aching from maintaining the pleasant expression. But I was constantly aware of my surroundings, of who was watching, of who might be the sender of those texts.

"Miss Griffen! Dora Lee!"

I turned to see Valentina Rossi herself pushing through the crowd. She was young, maybe thirty, with dark hair and striking features. Her eyes were bright with excitement.

"I can't believe you came! Isabella told me, but I thought maybe she was joking." She took both my hands, and I had to force myself not to pull away. "Your work has been such an inspiration to me. I studied your 1987 collection at Parsons. It changed everything for me, the way you used color and texture. It's one of the reasons I became a designer."

"That's very kind of you to say. Your show was wonderful. You have real talent."

"Thank you. That means everything coming from you." She glanced down at Pippa. "And she's adorable! Please, you have to come to the after-party. I want to introduce you to everyone."

Before I could politely decline, she'd linked her arm through mine and was guiding me toward the party space.

I was too tired to resist. Too overwhelmed. And maybe, just maybe, the person who'd sent those texts would reveal themselves at the party.

The after-party was in full swing, with servers circulating champagne and elaborate hors d'oeuvres. The room was packed with the same crowd from the show, now in a more relaxed, social mode.

Valentina introduced me to what felt like a hundred people. Editors, buyers, other designers, influencers, all wanting to meet the "legendary Dora Lee Griffen."

My face hurt from smiling. My feet screamed in the heels. My body begged for rest.

But I performed. I smiled. I chatted. I played the role.

Pippa was a hit, as always. People kept stopping to admire her outfit, and she basked in the attention, doing her tricks for treats that materialized from various pockets. At least she was enjoying herself.

I was talking to a young designer about fabric sources, my words automatic, when I felt someone watching me. The sensation was so strong it made my skin crawl.

I turned to see Milo standing alone near the bar, a drink in his hand, staring at me.

Our eyes met. He didn't look away. Didn't pretend he wasn't watching. Just stared, his face expressionless.

My breath caught in my throat. But I couldn't show fear. Couldn't let him see that he'd rattled me.

I excused myself from the young designer and made my way over to him, my legs unsteady but my chin up.

"Milo. Enjoying the party?"

"Not really." He took a sip of his drink, his eyes never leaving my face. "You know, I keep seeing you everywhere lately. Lawrence's presentation. The hospital visiting Jamie. Now here."

"It's a small industry."

"That's what I keep telling myself." He swirled his drink slowly, deliberately. "But it's funny how our paths keep crossing. Almost like you're following me. Or maybe looking for something."

My heart hammered against my ribs. "I don't know what you mean."

"Don't you?" He leaned in slightly, and I caught the smell of whiskey. "You're investigating. Asking questions. Poking around in things that don't concern you."

"I live in the building where someone died. It concerns me."

"Does it?" His smile didn't reach his eyes. "Or are you just a nosy old lady who should mind her own business?"

The words stung, but I kept my face neutral. "Perhaps I am."

"Then perhaps you should stop. Before you find something you don't want to find." He drained his glass. "Or before someone stops you."

Before I could respond, Lawrence appeared at his elbow.

"Milo, there you are. The buyer from Saks wants to talk about the fall collection." Lawrence noticed me and his smile tightened, annoyance flickering across his face. "Miss Griffen. What a surprise to see you here. Again."

The emphasis on that last word was unmistakable.

"I could say the same."

"Yes, well, we support up-and-coming talent when we can." He put his hand on Milo's shoulder in a gesture that looked friendly but seemed possessive, controlling. "We should go. They're waiting."

Milo shot me one last look, something unreadable in his eyes. Warning? Threat? Fear?

Then he let himself be led away.

I stood there, my hands trembling, trying to catch my breath. Milo had essentially threatened me. In a room full of people. And no one had noticed.

"Quite a crowd tonight."

The voice came from directly behind me, so close I could feel breath on my neck.

I turned to find Viola standing there, having appeared as if from nowhere. A trick she'd always been good at. Appearing exactly where she wanted to be, exactly when she wanted to be there.

And for a moment, time seemed to stop.

Because there she was. Tall. Five-eight, maybe five-nine in her heels. Slender. Well dressed in a black dress with dramatic sleeves, expensive fabric, perfect tailoring. Sophisticated. Polished. Every inch the successful designer.

Her platinum blonde hair was styled perfectly, catching the light.

But Marco had said dark hair. Shoulder length. Dark.

I've known Viola for forty years. I'd known her when her hair was that deep brunette, rich and dark, before she went platinum in her sixties. The height was right. The build was right. The sophisticated polish, the expensive taste.

It could have been her.

My stomach turned over, but I kept my face neutral. Forty years of competing in the fashion industry had taught me how to school my features. How to smile when I wanted to scream. How to shake hands with people I didn't trust.

How to have dinner with potential enemies and call them friends.

I studied her face, trying to see her as Marco had described. Looking for any sign. Any tell.

"Vi." My voice came out steadier than I felt. "I was wondering if you'd be here."

"I wouldn't miss it. Valentina is very talented." She sipped her champagne, her eyes on my face. Watching. Always watching. Cataloging every micro-expression, every shift in posture. "Though I'm surprised to see you here. I thought you'd sworn off these events."

A test. She wanted to know why I'd come. What I was doing here. Who I'd talked to.

"Isabella Benedetti got me on the list. Her husband owns Piccolo's."

I said it deliberately. Dropped the name like a stone into still water, then watched for the ripples.

And there it was. Just for a second. Something in her eyes. Her hand tightened almost imperceptibly on her champagne glass.

"Piccolo's," she said slowly, and I heard the calculation in her voice. How much did I know? What had Marco told me? "That's the Italian place on Spring Street, isn't it?"

"Yes. Have you been?"

Play innocent. Let her think I was just making conversation.

"Once or twice. Good food." Her voice was casual, but her eyes were sharp. Too sharp. "Why were you there?"

There. The real question. Not just casual interest. She needed to know.

"I heard Ethan used to eat there. Thought I'd try it."

"Hmm." She set her champagne glass down on a passing server's tray. Buying herself a moment. "And? Was it good?"

"Excellent. Marco, the owner, was very friendly. Very talkative." I paused deliberately. "He had some interesting stories about the regulars."

I watched her face. Watched for any sign that she knew what I was really saying.

She stepped closer, closing the distance between us, her movements deliberate. Controlled. "You know, Dora Lee, you've been asking a lot of questions lately. Stirring up a lot of dust."

"Have I?"

"People are talking. They're wondering why you're so interested in Ethan Kemper's death." She leaned in, and I had to force myself not to step back. "Some people are getting nervous."

My mouth went dry. "What people?"

"Just people." She touched my arm, and I felt my muscles tense beneath her fingers. "I'm your friend. I'm trying to protect you. But you need to stop this investigation before you get hurt."

I studied her face. This woman I'd known for forty years. This woman who'd been at my mother's funeral, who'd celebrated my successes and commiserated over my failures. This woman I'd competed against, circled around, never quite trusted.

This woman who might have met secretly with Ethan Kemper three weeks before he died.

"Is that a threat, Vi?"

"It's a warning." Her grip on my arm tightened. Not enough to hurt, but enough to make a point. "From someone who cares about you."

Cares about me. The phrase rang hollow. Did Viola care about anyone beyond herself? Beyond what they could do for her?

She held my gaze for a long moment, and I saw the calculation there. The assessment. She was trying to figure out how much I knew. How close I was to something she didn't want discovered.

After forty years of this dance, I recognized the look. It was the same one she'd given me on runways, at industry events, during every interaction where something important was at stake.

It was the look of a chess player who'd just realized her opponent might be better than she'd thought.

"Now, I should go mingle." She released my arm, and I felt the blood rush back to where her fingers had been. "But think about what I said, Dora Lee. Really think about it."

It sounded like advice. But it felt like a command.

She walked away, her black dress swishing, her platinum hair catching the light. Several people stopped her to chat, to compliment, to network. And she was gracious with all of them. Warm. Charming. The successful designer everyone wanted to know.

But I'd seen behind that mask. Just for a moment. I'd seen the calculation. The threat.

And I stood there, my heart pounding, my mind racing.

The woman at Piccolo's. Tall, slender, dark hair, wearing sunglasses at night to hide her identity. Meeting with Ethan three weeks before he died. Arguing about a broken promise.

It could have been Viola.

The height was right. The build was right. She'd had dark hair for most of her life. And she knew Milo well. Had talked to him for years. Had understood his frustrations. Had maybe encouraged them.

What if Viola had promised Ethan something? A collaboration? A mentorship? Access to her connections? And then broken that promise, choosing Milo instead?

What if she'd been playing both sides? Talking to Ethan while encouraging Milo's resentment? Setting them against each other?

I thought about dinner last week. How she'd steered the conversation. How she'd pushed suspicion toward Jamie. How she'd wanted to know exactly what I'd told the police.

How she'd warned me to stop investigating.

Forty years. We'd known each other for forty years.

And I still didn't know if I could trust her.

Worse, I was starting to think the answer was no.

I looked around the room. At Lawrence, chatting with buyers, his smile confident and cold. At Milo, standing silently beside him, looking trapped and miserable. At Viola, now talking to Valentina with a warm smile, all traces of threat gone from her face.

And at all the other faces. People I didn't know. People who might have sent those texts. People who might want me to stop investigating.

Two warnings in one night. The texts telling me to leave. Milo's thinly veiled threat. Viola's concerned warning that felt like something more sinister.

Someone was very worried about what I might discover.

Which meant I was close. Very close.

But close to what? Close to the truth? Or close to making a fatal mistake?

I needed to figure out the last piece of the puzzle. Who had met Ethan at Piccolo's three weeks before his death? Who had promised him something and then broken that promise?

And how did Milo fit into all of this? And Lawrence? And possibly Viola?

One of them was a killer.

And I was surrounded by all of them, alone except for Pippa, in a room full of people who couldn't help me if something happened.

I looked down at my elegant dress, my beautiful shoes, my carefully applied makeup. The armor I'd put on tonight.

But underneath, I was just a terrified seventy-eight-year-old woman who was in way over her head.

And I had no idea how to get out.

Somewhere in this room, or somewhere in this industry, was a killer. Someone who'd orchestrated Ethan's death. Someone who'd tried to kill Jamie. Someone who'd broken into my apartment.

I'd spent the past two weeks assuming it was Milo acting alone, or maybe Milo and Lawrence together.

But what if there was a third player? Someone who'd set everything in motion and then stepped back to watch it unfold?

Someone smart enough, calculating enough, patient enough to manipulate people like chess pieces?

I thought about Viola's question earlier. "Are you investigating or something?"

She'd known. She'd known from the very beginning that I was looking into Ethan's death.

And she'd been watching me ever since. Steering me. Warning me. Testing me.

Keep your friends close and your enemies closer.

But what do you do when you can't tell which one they are?

Chapter Nineteen

The car ride home from the Bowery Hotel felt longer than usual. My body ached with exhaustion. Hours of standing in heels, forcing smiles, maintaining that elegant facade while terror churned underneath. My makeup felt heavy on my skin. My feet screamed with every small movement.

I was running on nothing. Less than nothing.

My mind kept spinning through everything that had happened. The threatening texts. Caroline's warning. Viola's pointed conversation about Piccolo's, that flicker in her eyes when I mentioned it. Lawrence's obvious annoyance. Milo's thinly veiled threat: "Before someone stops you."

Someone was very worried about what I knew. Or what I was about to figure out.

Pippa dozed in my lap, exhausted from all the attention she'd received. I stroked her soft fur, trying to calm my racing thoughts, but my hands wouldn't stop shaking.

When we pulled up to the Royal Griffen, I thanked the driver and made my way inside. The lobby was quiet at this hour, almost midnight. Jerry was at the front desk, watching something on a small television.

"Evening, Miss Dora Lee," he said, standing up. "Big night out?"

"Fashion show. It ran late." My voice sounded strange to my own ears. Hollow.

"You look very fancy. And Miss Pippa too."

I tried to smile. "Thank you, Jerry. Have a good night."

"You too, Miss Dora Lee."

The elevator ride up to the tenth floor felt eternal. My feet hurt in the heels. My back ached. The elegant gown that had made me feel powerful now felt like a costume I couldn't wait to take off.

The hallway was silent as I approached my door. I fumbled in my clutch for my keys with trembling fingers, finally finding them.

But when I tried to insert the key into the lock, the door swung open.

It was already unlocked.

My heart stopped. I stood frozen in the doorway, staring into my dark apartment.

Something was wrong. Very wrong.

I reached inside and flipped on the light.

The sight that greeted me made my breath catch.

My apartment had been destroyed.

From where I stood, I could see the furniture overturned, cushions slashed open with stuffing spilling out like guts. Books had been swept from shelves, scattered across the floor. My sewing table, the one I'd used for fifty years, was on its side. My mannequins had been knocked over, the clothing I'd been working on trampled.

"No," I whispered.

Pippa whined at my feet, sensing something was wrong.

I immediately scooped her up, holding her against my chest. Glass. There would be glass everywhere. I couldn't let her cut her paws.

I stepped inside carefully, my heels crunching on something that scattered across the floor. Glass. I'd been right.

This wasn't just my apartment. This was my childhood home. The place where I'd grown up. Where I'd learned to sew at my mother's side. Where my father had told me stories about the hotel's grand opening. Where I'd spent every single day of my seventy-eight years.

And someone had violated it.

I moved through the living room, Pippa trembling in my arms. In the kitchen, cabinets hung open, dishes smashed on the floor in glittering shards. The contents of my refrigerator had been dumped out, food and milk pooling on the tiles.

My chest tightened.

I turned toward my desk. The legal pad, my legal pad with all my notes about the investigation, was gone. I looked around frantically. The plastic bag with the threatening note I'd received, gone. The photos I'd printed out, gone.

Someone had torn through my home, destroying everything, looking for my evidence.

And they'd found it.

All my work. All my notes. Everything I'd discovered.

Gone.

The room tilted violently. My chest hurt. Really hurt. Like someone was squeezing my heart in a vise.

Each breath came harder than the last. Too fast. Too shallow.

I needed to get out. I needed to get help. I needed to—

I turned back toward the door, but my legs wouldn't work properly. The elegant gown tangled around my ankles. My heels caught on something.

"Help," I tried to say, but no sound came. My throat had closed up.

Pippa squirmed in my arms, whining. I held her tighter, trying to reach the hallway, trying to get to safety, but I only made it a few steps.

My knees buckled.

I crumpled to the floor near the doorway, still clutching Pippa. My elegant gown pooled around me. The pain in my chest radiated down my left arm.

This was bad. This was very bad.

The edges of my vision started to go dark, closing in like a tunnel.

Pippa wriggled free and started barking frantically, her high-pitched yips piercing through the roaring in my ears. She was in the hallway now, barking and barking, the sound echoing off the walls.

And then, mercifully, I heard footsteps pounding down the hallway.

"Miss Dora Lee?" Jerry's voice, panicked. "Miss Dora Lee!"

I felt hands on my shoulders. Jerry's worried face swam into view above me, distorted, like looking through water.

"Call 911!" he shouted to someone. "Now!"

I tried to speak, to tell him I was okay, but I couldn't form words. The pain in my chest was overwhelming, radiating down my left arm.

More footsteps. More voices. Chelsea appeared, still in her work clothes even at this late hour, her face pale with shock.

"Oh my God. What happened?"

"I don't know. I heard the dog barking and came up to check. Her apartment, someone broke in." Jerry was on his phone now, his voice shaking. "Yes, tenth floor, apartment 1001. She's conscious but she's having some kind of medical episode. Chest pain, difficulty breathing. Please hurry."

Pippa pressed against me, whining. I tried to reach for her but my arm felt too heavy, like it was made of lead.

"It's okay, Miss Dora Lee. Help is coming." Chelsea knelt beside me, taking my hand. Hers was warm. Mine was ice cold. "Just breathe. Slow breaths."

I tried. I really tried. But everything hurt and I was so scared and my home was destroyed and all my evidence was gone and someone had done this and they'd been in my space, touching my things, destroying everything I loved, and what if they came back, what if they hurt Pippa, what if—

"The ambulance is on the way," Jerry said. "Five minutes."

Those five minutes felt like hours. Chelsea stayed with me, holding my hand, talking to me in a soothing voice about nothing important, just filling the silence. Jerry stood guard at the door, his body blocking the entrance, making sure whoever had done this didn't come back.

And Pippa never left my side, her warm little body pressed against mine, her tongue licking my hand over and over.

Finally, I heard sirens. Footsteps thundering up the stairs because the elevator was too slow.

Paramedics burst into the apartment, their faces professional and calm, a sharp contrast to Jerry and Chelsea's panic.

"Ma'am, can you hear me? I'm going to help you, okay?"

They checked my vital signs, their hands efficient and gentle. Asked me questions I could barely answer through the fog. Put an oxygen mask over my face, and the cool flow of air was a relief. Loaded me onto a stretcher, and I felt myself lifted, floating.

As they wheeled me toward the elevator, I grabbed Jerry's sleeve with what little strength I had left.

"Pippa," I managed to say through the mask, my voice muffled. "What about Pippa?"

"Don't worry, Miss Dora Lee." Jerry's kind face looked down at me, and I could see tears in his eyes. "We'll take care of her. I promise. You just focus on getting better."

"I'll keep her in my apartment tonight," Chelsea added, her voice thick. "She'll be safe, I promise. No one will hurt her."

The elevator doors closed, and I was carried down, out through the lobby where a few sleepy residents had gathered to see what was happening, their faces shocked and concerned, and into the waiting ambulance.

The ride to the hospital was a blur of beeping machines and concerned voices. I tried to stay calm, tried to breathe normally like they kept telling me to, but the panic kept threatening to overwhelm me.

Someone had been in my home. Someone had destroyed everything. Someone wanted to scare me badly enough that they'd violated my most private space.

And it had worked. I was terrified.

But underneath the fear, underneath the pain, something else was growing.

Anger.

How dare they. How dare they come into my home, destroy my things, try to intimidate me.

I'd lived in that building for seventy-eight years. I'd survived my parents' deaths, the hotel closing, decades of ups and downs in the fashion industry, and I'd be damned if some murderer was going to scare me out of my own home.

By the time we reached the hospital, my chest pain had eased slightly. The oxygen was helping. My mind was clearing, sharpening with rage.

They wheeled me into the emergency room, and a doctor appeared, young and competent-looking, asking questions, running tests, hooking me up to monitors that beeped and whirred.

"Your heart rhythm is irregular," he said, studying a screen. "Could be stress-induced. We're going to keep you overnight for observation, run some more tests in the morning."

"I need to go home."

"Not tonight, Miss Griffen. You've had a significant episode. We need to make sure you're stable."

I wanted to argue, but I was so tired. So, bone-deep exhausted. My body had finally reached its limit.

They moved me to a room, got me settled in a bed. A nurse brought me water and adjusted my monitors, the machines still beeping their steady rhythm.

"Try to get some rest," she said kindly, dimming the lights. "Your body needs it."

After she left, I lay there in the dark, staring at the ceiling. The room was quiet except for the beeping of the heart monitor and the occasional sound of footsteps in the hallway outside.

My mind wouldn't stop working. Couldn't stop.

Who had done this? Who had broken into my apartment?

Milo. Just hours ago at the fashion show, he'd essentially threatened me. "Before you find something you don't want to find. Or before someone stops you."

Had he left the party right after I did? Had he gotten to the Royal Griffen before me and torn through my apartment looking for evidence?

Or Lawrence. He'd been annoyed to see me at the show. Annoyed that I kept appearing at industry events, asking questions. He had the most to lose if I discovered his connection to the murder.

Or even Viola. She'd warned me to stop investigating. She'd seemed nervous when I mentioned Piccolo's. What if she'd been the woman in the restaurant? What if she'd broken into my apartment to destroy any evidence connecting her to Ethan?

I'd felt watched at Carlo's Market. Someone had sent me threatening texts during the show. And now someone had destroyed my home.

This wasn't random. This was planned. Deliberate.

Someone was very, very worried about what I knew.

The anger burned brighter, pushing away the fear.

They'd violated my childhood home. Destroyed seventy-eight years of memories. Tried to scare me into silence.

But they'd made a mistake.

They'd shown me just how desperate they were. Which meant I was close. Very close to the truth.

And once I got out of this hospital, I was going to—

Wait.

I sat up slightly, my heart rate picking up. The monitor beeped faster.

The photos.

The printed photos were gone. My notes were gone.

But the originals.

The originals were still on my phone.

My phone. In my clutch. Which should be... where?

I looked around frantically. There, on the small table beside the bed. My silver clutch, placed there by one of the paramedics or nurses.

I reached for it with shaking hands, nearly knocking over the water cup. Opened it. And there it was.

My phone.

With trembling fingers, I unlocked it and went to my photos. Scrolled back through the recent ones. The fashion show. Pippa in her silver outfit. And then, further back.

There.

The letter signed "L." The calendar with "2pm - LJ" written on the day Ethan died. The maintenance keycard in Milo's gym bag. The sketches showing Milo's contributions to Ethan's designs.

All of it. Still here. Still safe.

I let out a breath I hadn't realized I'd been holding. Relief washed over me so powerfully that tears stung my eyes.

They hadn't won. They'd destroyed my notes, taken my printed photos, violated my home.

But they hadn't gotten the originals.

I still had evidence. Real evidence. Evidence that proved Milo had been in contact with Lawrence. Evidence that proved Milo had access to a maintenance keycard that would have let him move through the building undetected.

I lay back against the pillows, clutching my phone to my chest like a lifeline.

Tomorrow, I would deal with the police. I would show them these photos. I would tell them everything I knew.

Tomorrow, I would call Detective Keller and make sure she understood that Milo Savage was dangerous. That he'd threatened me. That he'd probably broken into my apartment.

Tomorrow, I would figure out if Viola was involved. If she was the woman from Piccolo's. If my oldest friend had been lying to me for weeks.

But tonight, I just needed to survive. To rest. To let my battered body recover.

I thought about Pippa, safe with Chelsea. About Jerry standing guard at my door. About the community in the Royal Griffen that had come together to help me.

About how much I had to lose if I didn't stop this killer.

And about how much I had to fight for.

Whoever had broken into my apartment had made a critical mistake. They'd thought destroying my physical notes would stop me.

But I was Dora Lee Griffen. I'd spent seventy-eight years in that building. I'd survived loss and heartbreak and the slow decline of my career.

And I'd survived tonight.

The anger settled into something harder. Something determined.

They'd shown their hand. They'd revealed just how desperate they were.

Which meant I was closer to the truth than I'd realized.

And once I got out of this hospital, I was going to finish what I'd started.

I had the photos. I had the evidence.

And I had nothing left to lose.

No matter what it took, I was going to catch this killer.

Even if it killed me.

Chapter Twenty

I didn't sleep well. Every time I started to drift off, I'd jerk awake, my heart racing, reliving the moment I'd walked into my destroyed apartment.

The nurses came in regularly to check on me, take my vitals, ask how I was feeling. Each time, I said I was fine, even though I wasn't.

One nurse adjusted the IV drip in my arm. "This is just fluids," she explained. "You were dehydrated when you came in. We want to make sure you're properly hydrated before discharge."

I hadn't even noticed how thirsty I'd been. Too focused on everything else.

Around six in the morning, I gave up on sleep entirely. I sat up in bed, reaching for the small bag of personal items they'd brought up from the ER. My clutch, my phone, my jewelry.

My phone.

I needed to back up the photos. If something happened to my phone, I'd lose everything.

I spent the next hour creating a cloud backup, emailing the most important photos to myself, making sure the evidence existed in multiple places. The killer had destroyed my physical notes, but they wouldn't get these.

Writing everything down had just been to keep my hands busy while my mind worked anyway. I remembered every conversation, every clue, every suspicion. The legal pad had been a tool for thinking, not for memory.

The morning passed slowly. Blood tests, an EKG, questions from various doctors and nurses. They all seemed satisfied that my episode had been stress-induced and that my heart was fundamentally sound.

"You're very lucky, Miss Griffen," the cardiologist said. "But you need to take it easy. Less stress. More rest. At your age, these kinds of episodes can be serious."

"I understand."

"I'm serious. If you keep pushing yourself, next time could be worse." He glanced at my chart. "You were also dehydrated, which doesn't help. Are you eating regularly? Drinking enough water?"

"I've been... busy."

"Too busy to take care of yourself?" He gave me a stern look over his reading glasses. "Miss Griffen, your body is telling you to slow down. Please listen to it."

"I'll be more careful."

He didn't look convinced, but he signed my discharge papers.

A nurse came in about an hour later. "Good news, Miss Griffen. The doctor has signed your discharge papers. We'll just need to get a few things in order. First, do you have a ride home?"

"I can call someone. Our building housekeeper has a car."

"Perfect. Go ahead and give her a call, and we'll finish up your paperwork while we wait for her."

I found Georgie's number in my phone and called.

"Hello?"

"Georgie, it's Dora Lee. I'm so sorry to bother you, but I'm at Mount Sinai hospital and I need a ride home. The nurses won't let me leave without someone to pick me up."

"Miss Dora Lee! Of course I'll come get you. I'm just finishing up my last cleaning of the day. Give me about an hour?"

"That would be perfect. Thank you so much."

"Don't you even worry about it. I'm happy to help." Her voice was warm, reassuring. "Jerry told me what happened last night. We've all been so worried about you. How are you feeling?"

"Better. They're discharging me, so I must be okay."

"Well, you just sit tight. I'll be there as soon as I can. And don't worry about Pippa, she's been with me and she's doing just fine."

"Thank you, Georgie. For everything."

"That's what family does, honey. See you soon."

True to her word, Georgie arrived almost exactly an hour later. She came bustling into my room, still in her work clothes, her face etched with concern.

"Miss Dora Lee! Look at you, sitting up and looking better already."

"I'm alright. Really."

"You gave us all such a scare last night." She took my arm gently. "Come on, let's get you home."

The nurse helped me into the wheelchair, even though I insisted I could walk. Hospital policy, she said.

Georgie pushed me out to the parking lot, chatting the whole way about her day, her boys, her mother, clearly trying to keep things light and normal.

Her car was an older sedan, clean but well-used. She helped me into the passenger seat with surprising gentleness for someone who spent her days lifting heavy cleaning equipment.

As we pulled out of the parking lot, Georgie glanced over at me.

"So. You want to tell me what really happened?"

"Someone broke into my apartment while I was at a fashion show last night. Destroyed everything. Looking for something."

"Looking for what?"

"Evidence. I've been investigating Ethan Kemper's murder."

Georgie was quiet for a moment, navigating through traffic. Then she sighed.

"I knew you were up to something. All those questions you've been asking. But Miss Dora Lee, this is dangerous. Someone killed that boy, and now they've gone after you."

"I know."

"Jerry called the police right away last night. Detective Keller came by this morning. She looked at your apartment, took photos, dusted for fingerprints. She wanted to talk to you, but the hospital said you needed rest."

"What did she say? About the break-in?"

"That it was clearly targeted. Whoever did it was looking for something specific. They didn't take your TV or your jewelry or any of the obvious valuable things. They just tore through everything."

We drove in silence for a few minutes. I watched the city pass by, thinking about what Georgie had said.

"How's Pippa?" I asked suddenly.

"She's fine. Chelsea kept her last night like she promised, gave her treats and lots of cuddles. Then I took her this morning when I was cleaning the building. She's at my place right now with my boys. They're spoiling her rotten. David's been teaching her a new trick."

"Thank you. I was so worried about her."

"She's safe. And she'll be happy to see you." Georgie paused. "Miss Dora Lee, can I ask you something?"

"Of course."

"Why are you doing this? Investigating a murder? You're not a detective. You're a fashion designer. Why put yourself in danger?"

It was a fair question. One I'd been asking myself.

"Because Ethan deserves justice. Because I don't think the police are looking at the right people. And because..." I trailed off, trying to find the right words. "Because I'm good at it. At seeing things others miss. At putting pieces together. And because someone threatened me, and I don't respond well to threats."

Georgie laughed at that. "No, I don't imagine you do."

"Plus, I live in that building. If there's a murderer walking around, I want to know who it is."

"That's fair." She turned onto my street. "So, do you know? Who killed him?"

"I have theories. But I need proof. Real proof."

"And you think you had that proof in your apartment? The stuff that got stolen?"

"Some of it. But not all of it." I pulled out my phone. "I still have photos. Evidence. Things the killer doesn't know I have."

"Good. That's good." She pulled up in front of the Royal Griffen. "Okay, let's get you upstairs."

Walter rushed to open the door when he saw us.

"Miss Dora Lee! You're back! How are you feeling?"

"I'm fine, Walter. A bit tired, but fine."

"We were all so worried. Such a terrible thing, someone breaking in like that."

Georgie helped me into the lobby. Chelsea appeared from her office, relief evident on her face.

"Dora Lee, thank goodness. Are you alright?"

"Yes. The doctors said I just need rest."

"I've had the locks changed on your apartment," Chelsea said. "And we've added additional security measures. This won't happen again."

"Thank you. And thank you for taking care of Pippa last night."

"Of course. She's a sweet girl. Slept right on my bed." Chelsea smiled. "Detective Keller wants to speak with you when you're feeling up to it. She left her card."

"I'll call her."

Georgie and I took the elevator up to the tenth floor. When we reached my door, with its shiny new lock, I hesitated.

"You want me to go in first?" Georgie asked gently.

"No. I need to see it."

I unlocked the door and pushed it open.

Someone had cleaned. Not everything was fixed, but the broken glass had been swept up, the overturned furniture righted, the worst of the damage cleared away.

It still looked like a disaster, but it was manageable. Livable.

"Jerry and I did what we could this morning," Georgie said. "We didn't want you coming home to the full mess. But your personal things, we didn't touch those. Didn't know what you'd want to keep or throw away." She squeezed my shoulder. "But I'm happy to help so you don't overexert yourself. Just let me know when you're ready and I'll be here. I'll bring my boys. They need to keep busy with something."

"Oh, Georgie, you don't have to—"

"I know I don't have to. I want to." Her tone left no room for argument. "You're family, Miss Dora Lee. We take care of family. Now, you sit down while I go get Pippa. She's been missing you."

Georgie left, and I stood in the middle of my apartment, looking at the damage.

My beautiful home. My sanctuary. Violated.

But I was still here. I was still standing.

And I was going to find out who did this.

Fifteen minutes later, Georgie returned with Pippa, who launched herself at me with such enthusiasm that I nearly fell over.

"Pippa! Oh, sweet girl, I missed you too."

She licked my face, her tail wagging so hard her whole body shook. I held her close, feeling the tight knot in my chest finally start to loosen.

"She wouldn't eat much this morning," Georgie said, setting a covered dish on my kitchen counter. "I think she was worried about you. Oh, and I brought you some chicken soup. My mama's recipe. It'll help you get your strength back."

"Georgie, you didn't have to—"

"Course I did. You need to eat, and I know you're not going to feel like cooking tonight." She pulled out a spoon from my drawer. "At least have a little now while it's still warm."

I was about to protest, but my stomach growled loudly. I couldn't remember the last time I'd eaten.

"Okay. Thank you."

She ladled out a bowl and I took a sip. It was perfect. Rich and comforting, exactly what I needed.

"This is delicious."

"Good. There's plenty more for later." She watched me eat a few more spoonfuls, then nodded with satisfaction. "Alright, I should get home. My boys are probably wondering where I am. But you call me tomorrow, or the next day, whenever you're ready, and we'll come help you sort through everything."

"I will. Thank you, Georgie. For everything."

Her eyes got a little misty at that. "Always, honey. Always."

After she left, I sat on my couch with Pippa curled up beside me, finishing the soup. The warmth spread through me, and I felt more human than I had since walking into this destroyed apartment.

I looked around at the damage. The slashed cushions. The scattered books. The overturned table.

The killer had made a mistake. They'd shown me just how desperate they were. How threatened they felt.

I pulled out my phone and started going through the photos again, making mental notes to recreate what I'd lost.

Tomorrow, I would talk to Detective Keller. Tell her everything I knew.

But tonight, I just needed to rest. To recover. To plan.

Because this wasn't over.

Not by a long shot.

Chapter Twenty-One

I woke to pale morning light filtering through my curtains and Pippa's wet nose pressed against my cheek. For a moment, I forgot where I was. Then the ache in my body reminded me. The hospital. The break-in. Coming home to find my life scattered across the floor.

I was on the couch, still in the clothes Georgie had brought me at the hospital. I must have fallen asleep here last night after she left, too exhausted to even change.

"Good morning, sweet girl," I murmured, scratching behind Pippa's ears. She wagged her tail and licked my face, clearly relieved I was still here.

Slowly, I pushed myself upright. Every muscle protested. My chest still felt tight from whatever had happened last night, that moment of panic that had sent me to the floor.

I looked around at my apartment in the daylight. The damage was still there, of course, but somehow it looked more manageable than it had last night. Less like a violation and more like a mess that could be cleaned up. Georgie and Jerry had done good work.

I shuffled to the kitchen and made coffee, grateful that the intruder hadn't destroyed my coffee maker. Small mercies. I found some crackers in a cabinet that hadn't been ransacked and nibbled on them while the coffee brewed.

My phone sat on the counter where I'd left it. I picked it up and saw the notification. Detective Keller had called while I was asleep.

I'd call her back. But first, coffee.

I was halfway through my first cup when my phone rang. Detective Keller again.

"Miss Griffen, I heard you were released from the hospital. How are you feeling?"

"Better, thank you."

"I need to come by and talk to you about the break-in. Get your statement. Would this afternoon work?"

"That would be fine."

"Good. I'll be there around two." She paused. "Miss Griffen, I also need to talk to you about your investigation into Ethan Kemper's death."

My stomach dropped. "My investigation?"

"We found evidence in your apartment that you've been looking into the case on your own. Notes, photos. The perpetrator took most of it, but there were some scraps left behind." Her tone was stern. "We need to discuss this."

"I understand."

"See you at two."

After we hung up, I sat there holding my coffee, thinking. Detective Keller knew I'd been investigating. She was going to tell me to stop, to leave it to the professionals.

But I couldn't stop. Not now. Not when I was so close.

Around eleven, there was a knock at my door. I looked through the peephole, my heart racing.

It was Jamie Patton.

She was still bruised, her arm in a sling, but she was out of the hospital and standing on her own two feet.

I opened the door. "Jamie. What are you doing here?"

"I heard what happened. That someone broke into your apartment." She shifted uncomfortably, and I noticed she was holding a small bouquet of flowers in her good hand. "Can I come in?"

"Of course."

She stepped inside and handed me the flowers. "These are for you. You brought me flowers in the hospital, and I wanted to return the kindness."

"Oh, Jamie. You didn't have to do that."

"I wanted to." She looked around at the damage. "Oh my God. This is awful."

"It's better than it was. Some friends helped clean up."

We sat down, Pippa immediately going over to sniff Jamie's shoes. Jamie smiled and petted her gently with her good hand.

"I wanted to thank you," Jamie said. "For visiting me in the hospital. For the flowers. For believing me when I said someone tried to kill me."

"Of course I believed you."

"The police didn't. They still think it was just an accident, that I stepped into traffic." She looked at me with serious eyes. "But you and I both know better, don't we? Someone came after both of us."

"Yes."

"Which means we're on the same side. We're both trying to figure out who killed Ethan." She took a breath. "And I want to help. I want to clear my name because I know people think I did it."

"Do you have an alibi? For the day Ethan died?"

"Yes. I was at a casting call in Brooklyn. From noon until almost five. There were dozens of people there, photographers, other models, the casting director. I can give you names, prove I was there." She pulled out her phone. "I even have photos from that day, time-stamped. See?"

She showed me her phone. Sure enough, there were selfies and candid shots from a casting call, all time-stamped between 12:30 and 4:45 pm.

The time of death window Detective Keller had mentioned was between two and five. Jamie couldn't have killed Ethan.

"Why didn't you tell the police this?"

"They never asked. They questioned me once, but it was just general questions about my relationship with Ethan, whether I knew of anyone who wanted to hurt him. They never asked where I was that specific day." She looked frustrated. "And by the time I realized I should tell them, they'd already moved on to other suspects."

"You should still tell them. Detective Keller is coming here this afternoon. You could come back then, give her this information."

"I will. I want to." She leaned forward. "Miss Dora Lee, I didn't kill Ethan. I was angry at him, bitter about being dropped, but I didn't want him dead. I just wanted him to see me, to remember that I existed, that I was good at what I did."

There was genuine pain in her voice. Genuine grief.

"I believe you, Jamie."

"Thank you." She wiped at her eyes with her good hand. "When I saw him at events after he dropped me, I'd try to catch his eye, try to remind him of the work we'd done together. But it was like I was invisible. Like I'd never mattered at all."

"That must have been very painful."

"It was. And I handled it badly. I know I did. The meltdowns, the bad-mouthing, all of it. I was just so hurt and I didn't know what else to do with that feeling." She looked around at my damaged apartment. "But someone killing him? And then trying to kill me? And breaking into your home? That's not about hurt feelings. That's about something much bigger."

"I think you're right."

"Do you know who did it? Who killed Ethan?"

"I have theories. But I need more proof before I can say anything."

Jamie nodded. "Well, whatever I can do to help, I will. Ethan didn't deserve what happened to him. No matter how he treated people, no matter his flaws, he didn't deserve to die like that."

We talked for a while longer. Jamie told me more about her time working with Ethan, the good moments before things went wrong. She talked about the casting call that day, how she'd been hopeful about booking the job, how she'd gotten the call about Ethan's death while she was on the subway home.

By the time she left, promising to return at two to talk to Detective Keller, I was convinced. Jamie Patton hadn't killed Ethan Kemper.

Which meant I could cross her off my suspect list.

That left Milo and Lawrence.

Or someone I hadn't even considered yet.

I spent the next few hours going through the photos on my phone again, making notes on my computer this time instead of on paper. Backing everything up to the cloud so it couldn't be stolen again.

The letter signed "L." The calendar marking. The maintenance keycard. The evidence of Milo's design contributions.

And the woman at Piccolo's. Tall, slender, dark hair, wearing sunglasses at night. Meeting with Ethan three weeks before his death.

"You promised me," Ethan had said.

What promise? What had someone promised him that they didn't deliver?

At two o'clock sharp, Detective Keller arrived. She looked tired, like she'd been working too many hours on too little sleep.

"Miss Griffen. May I come in?"

"Of course."

She stepped inside and looked around, her expression grim. "They really did a number on your place."

"It's better than it was."

"I saw the photos from this morning. I can only imagine." She pulled out a notebook. "Let's start with last night. Walk me through what happened."

I told her about the fashion show, coming home late, finding the door unlocked and the apartment destroyed.

"And you didn't see anyone? No one in the hallway or stairwell?"

"No. But I got threatening texts during the fashion show. From an unknown number."

Her head snapped up. "You did? Do you still have them?"

I pulled out my phone and showed her. Her expression darkened as she read them.

"Why didn't you call me immediately?"

"I should have. I'm sorry. I was trying to figure things out on my own."

"Miss Griffen, you can't investigate a murder on your own. It's dangerous. As evidenced by..." She gestured to my apartment. "This."

"I know. But I found things. Evidence that I don't think you have."

She looked at me for a long moment. "What kind of evidence?"

"Photos from inside Ethan and Milo's apartment."

"You broke into their apartment?"

I hesitated. "I accessed it through the building's old dumbwaiter system."

"When?"

"A few nights ago. I know I shouldn't have, but I needed to see if there was any evidence that might help."

She rubbed her temples. "Miss Griffen, that's breaking and entering. Trespassing. And any evidence you found could be considered tainted now. Do you understand how serious this is?"

"I do. And I'm sorry. But I didn't touch anything, didn't move anything. I just took photos."

"Just took photos," she repeated, her tone incredulous. "Of a suspect's private residence. Without a warrant. Without permission."

"Yes."

She looked like she wanted to arrest me on the spot, but instead she took a deep breath. "Show me what you found."

I showed her everything. The letter, the calendar, the keycard, the sketches. I explained what each one meant, how it all connected.

Detective Keller was quiet as she looked through each photo, making notes.

"This is good work," she admitted reluctantly. "This is actually very good work. But it's also very dangerous. Whoever killed Ethan Kemper knows you have this information now. That's why they broke in, why they threatened you."

"I know."

"Which means you need to step back. Let us handle it from here."

Before I could respond, there was another knock at my door.

Jamie had returned, as promised.

I introduced her to Detective Keller, and Jamie immediately launched into her alibi, showing the photos, giving names and contact information.

Detective Keller took it all down, her expression thoughtful.

"Thank you, Miss Patton. This is very helpful. I'll follow up with these contacts."

After Jamie left, Detective Keller turned back to me.

"So, if Jamie Patton didn't kill Ethan Kemper, who do you think did?"

"Based on the evidence? Milo Savage."

"That's been our working theory as well. The motive, the opportunity, the suspicious behavior. But we don't have enough to arrest him yet. We need something concrete."

"What if I could get him to confess?"

"Absolutely not. Miss Griffen, you're a civilian. You're not going to confront a potential murderer."

"But what if—"

"No." Her voice was firm. "You've done good work here. You've found evidence we didn't have. But now you need to let us do our job. Stay safe. Lock your doors. Don't go anywhere alone. And for God's sake, stop investigating."

After she left, I sat on my couch with Pippa, thinking.

Detective Keller was right. I should stop. I should let the professionals handle it.

But something still didn't add up.

If Milo had killed Ethan, why did he seem so miserable? Why did he keep insisting he didn't do it? Why was he trapped under Lawrence's thumb?

Unless Lawrence was involved too. Unless they'd planned it together and something had gone wrong.

Or unless someone else entirely was pulling the strings.

I looked at the photos again, focusing on the letter signed "L."

L for Lawrence? Or L for someone else?

My phone buzzed. A text from an unknown number.

"Stop now or the next time won't be a warning."

My hands shook as I read it. They were watching me. Still watching.

I stared at my phone screen, and that's when I noticed them. Three missed calls from Viola. Two voicemails. Several texts saying she'd heard about the break-in, asking if I was okay, wanting to know why I wasn't answering.

I hadn't responded to any of them. Hadn't even opened the texts.

Because I didn't know if I could trust her anymore.

Viola had been my friend for over forty years. We'd celebrated successes together, commiserated over failures. She'd been there through so much of my life.

But she'd also been so interested in steering my investigation. Pushing suspicion toward Jamie. Asking pointed questions about Piccolo's. Warning me to stop, over and over.

Was she protecting me? Or protecting herself?

I thought about the woman at Piccolo's. Tall, slender, dark hair, wearing sunglasses at night. Meeting secretly with Ethan three weeks before his death.

Viola was tall. Slender. She'd had dark hair for most of her life before going platinum.

Could it have been her?

"You promised me," Ethan had said to that woman.

What could Viola have promised Ethan? And why would she meet him in secret?

I looked at the threatening text again. "Stop now or the next time won't be a warning."

Viola had warned me. Multiple times. To stop investigating, to let it go, to stay safe.

Had those been genuine warnings from a concerned friend?

Or threats disguised as concern?

"I'm being paranoid," I said out loud to Pippa. "Viola wouldn't hurt me. She's my friend."

But was she?

I thought about how she'd mentioned Milo being her customer. How she'd known details about the case that seemed convenient. How she'd been so quick to redirect suspicion away from certain people and toward others.

Maybe I was being paranoid. Maybe forty years of friendship meant something.

Or maybe I'd been confiding in someone who had reasons to want me to stop digging.

I set my phone down without responding to Viola's messages. Not yet. Not until I knew for sure.

But I wasn't going to stop investigating.

I'd come too far to stop now.

Chapter Twenty-Two

The next morning, I woke up on my couch. I'd been too exhausted to make it to my bedroom, and honestly, the couch felt safer. Closer to the door. More aware of my surroundings.

Pippa was curled up against me, her warmth comforting. I stroked her soft fur, grateful for her presence.

My apartment looked even worse in the morning light. The damage was stark, unavoidable. But at least it was clean enough to be functional.

I made myself coffee and toast, moving slowly, still sore from the stress of the past several days. My phone rang just as I was settling back on the couch.

Viola.

I stared at the screen. Part of me wanted to let it go to voicemail like I had yesterday. But I couldn't avoid her forever. And maybe, in my exhausted state, I'd see something I'd missed before. Some tell. Some sign of whether she was friend or foe.

Or maybe I was just too tired to keep playing games.

I answered.

"Finally!" Viola's voice was a mix of relief and frustration. "I've been trying to reach you since yesterday morning. I heard about your apartment, the hospital, everything. Why didn't you call me back?"

The concern sounded genuine. But Viola had always been good at sounding genuine.

"It's been chaotic, Vi. I'm sorry."

"Chaotic, yes, but you scared me half to death. I left you three voicemails and I don't know how many texts." Her voice softened with what sounded like genuine worry. "I was about to come over and break down your door to make sure you were okay."

The concern in her voice sounded real. I could hear it, feel it through the phone. But was it? Or was I so exhausted that I couldn't tell anymore?

Forty years of knowing someone, and I still couldn't read her with certainty.

"I'm okay. Really."

"Are you though?" She paused, and I heard the assessment in that pause. "How bad is it? The apartment?"

What was she really asking? How much damage? What was taken? What evidence did I lose?

Or was I being paranoid again?

"Pretty bad. But I'm working on it."

"You shouldn't be there alone, surrounded by all that destruction. Let me take you out to lunch. Or dinner. Whichever you prefer. Get you away from that mess for a few hours."

The offer was kind. Thoughtful. Exactly what a good friend would suggest.

Or exactly what someone who wanted to see how much the break-in had rattled me would suggest.

I was too tired for this. Too exhausted to keep analyzing every word, every pause, every offer.

I hesitated. Part of me wanted to say no, to keep working, to maintain my distance. But another part of me was exhausted and hungry and tired of looking at the damage.

"Dinner would be nice."

"Perfect. How about Golden Dragon? That little Chinese place we used to go to?"

"I haven't been there in years."

"Neither have I. It'll be like old times. Let's say six o'clock?"

"I'll meet you there."

After we hung up, I looked down at Pippa. "What do you think, girl? Am I being paranoid?"

She tilted her head, ears flopping.

"You're right. Viola's been my friend for over forty years. Of course she's worried about me."

I spent the rest of the morning and early afternoon sorting through the damage, making piles of what could be salvaged and what needed to be thrown away. Some things were beyond repair, slashed cushions, torn fabric, shattered dishes. But I salvaged what I could. The work was therapeutic in a way, giving me something concrete to focus on.

Around three, I took a break to shower and get ready for dinner. I chose a simple black tunic over leggings, with a colorful silk scarf and my favorite silver earrings. Nothing too fancy, but put-together enough for dinner out.

I called for a car at five-thirty, arriving at Golden Dragon a few minutes before six. The restaurant was in Chinatown, a small family-owned place that had been there for decades. The décor was dated but charming, with red lanterns and gold dragons painted on the walls. The smell of garlic, ginger, and soy sauce filled the air.

Viola was already there, waiting at a corner table away from the other diners. She looked elegant as always in tailored slacks and a cashmere sweater. Put together. Controlled. Everything I wasn't right now.

She stood when she saw me and pulled me into a tight hug. "Oh, Dora Lee. I'm so glad you're okay. When I heard about the break-in and that you'd been hospitalized, I was terrified."

The embrace felt genuine. But I'd been fooled by genuine-feeling things before.

"I'm fine. Really."

She pulled back and looked at me critically, her eyes scanning my face like she was cataloging details. The exhaustion. The worry lines. How much this had affected me. "You look exhausted."

"I am exhausted."

"Then let's get you fed. Sit, sit." She gestured to the chair like she was taking care of me. Or like she wanted me settled where she could watch me. "You need to eat. Build your strength back up."

I sat, and Pippa immediately curled up at my feet. At least she trusted Viola.

That should mean something. Shouldn't it?

A waiter brought us tea and menus.

"I always get the same thing here," Viola said. "Kung Pao chicken and pork fried rice."

"I think I'll try the Mongolian beef. I haven't had that in forever."

A waiter brought us tea and menus. We ordered, and Viola poured us both tea from the small ceramic pot. The ritual was familiar, comforting. Forty years of dinners together had created its own rhythm.

"So," she said, wrapping her hands around her cup. Her listening posture. "Tell me everything. What happened?"

I gave her an edited version of the story. The fashion show, coming home to find the apartment destroyed, the medical episode, the hospital stay.

She listened without interrupting, her face a picture of concern. But I noticed her fingers tightening slightly on the teacup when I mentioned finding the apartment destroyed.

"And the police think this is connected to Ethan Kemper's death?"

"They do. Someone was looking for evidence I'd collected."

"Evidence?" The word came out carefully measured. "What have you been doing?"

There it was. The real question. Not just concern, but calculation. What did I know? What had I found? What had been taken?

"Asking questions. Looking into things. Trying to figure out what really happened."

"But why? Why would you put yourself in danger like that?" Her concern seemed authentic, her worry for me evident in every line of her face. But was she worried about me? Or about what I might have discovered?

"Because someone needed to."

She studied me across the table, and I saw the wheels turning behind her eyes. Assessing. Calculating how much I knew. How much danger I posed to whatever she was protecting.

Or maybe I was imagining it. Maybe exhaustion and paranoia were making me see threats everywhere.

She reached across the table and took my hand. "I know you. You've always been stubborn, always determined to get to the truth. But this time, you almost got killed. Someone broke into your home. They could have hurt you. They could have..." She trailed off, her grip tightening on my hand.

Our food arrived, and we ate in silence for a few minutes. The Kung Pao chicken was good. The Mongolian beef was better. But I barely tasted any of it.

"Are you sure you're okay?" Viola asked, studying my face. "You seem distant. Like you're holding something back."

Of course she'd noticed. Viola always noticed.

I forced a smile. "I'm just tired, Vi. It's been a long few days."

"I'm sure it has." She set down her chopsticks deliberately. "Have the police made any progress? Do they know who did it?"

I hesitated. Every word felt like a test. What to reveal? What to hold back? "There are still questions. They're investigating, but no proof yet."

"But they must have some suspects?"

"A few. But nothing concrete."

She studied me for a moment, and I saw frustration flicker across her face. I wasn't giving her what she wanted. Whatever that was.

"Well, I hope they figure it out soon. You shouldn't have to live with this hanging over you."

I hesitated, then decided to test her. Just a little. "I think there might have been more than one person involved. That someone else knew what was going to happen."

"Like who?" Too quick. Too interested.

"Lawrence Jung, maybe. The timing of everything, how quickly he moved in after Ethan died." I paused, watching her face. "And there's something else. Someone met Ethan at a restaurant three weeks before he died. A woman. She was wearing sunglasses at night, trying to hide her identity."

Her hand tightened imperceptibly on her chopsticks. Just for a second. Then she set them down with careful control.

"Do you know who it was?"

"No. But I'm trying to find out." I held her gaze. "The owner of the restaurant said she was tall. Slender. Dark hair. Very sophisticated. Expensive taste."

Something shifted in Viola's eyes. Recognition? Fear? Or was I imagining it?

"That could describe half the women in the fashion industry," she said lightly. But her voice had an edge to it that hadn't been there before.

"True." I took a sip of tea. "But how many of them would meet secretly with Ethan three weeks before he died? Wearing sunglasses inside at night to hide their identity?"

"I don't know, Dora Lee." She leaned back, and her expression had shifted from concern to something harder. "But I think you need to be very careful about what you're accusing people of. Very careful about connecting dots that might not actually connect."

Was that advice? Or a warning?

"I'm not accusing anyone. I'm just trying to understand what happened."

"Are you?" She picked up her tea, her movements precise. "Because from where I'm sitting, it sounds like you're building a theory. And theories can be dangerous when you don't have all the facts."

"I know."

We finished our meal, but the easy conversation never quite returned. The tension sat between us like a third person at the table.

Viola paid the check despite my protests. "My treat. You've been through enough."

Outside on the sidewalk, she pulled me into another hug. "Promise me you'll be careful. About the investigation. About what you're looking into."

"I'm always careful."

"Are you?" She pulled back, her hands still on my shoulders. "Because someone broke into your apartment, Dora Lee. They destroyed your home. They were looking for something. That's not the kind of person you want to make angry."

"I know."

"Do you?" Her grip tightened slightly. "Because I'm not sure you do. I'm not sure you understand how dangerous this is."

There was something in her eyes I couldn't quite read. Genuine fear for my safety? Or fear of something else?

Her car arrived first. She squeezed my hand once more. "Call me tomorrow. Let me know you're okay."

"I will."

She got in, and through the window I watched her immediately pull out her phone. Her face was serious, focused. She started typing something as the car pulled away.

Who was she texting? And why did she need to do it the moment she left me?

My ride pulled up a minute later, and I headed home.

In the car, I thought about dinner. About every word, every pause, every look.

Viola had been worried about me. I believed that much.

But she'd also been worried about what I knew. About that mysterious woman I'd described. About how close I was getting to something.

The way her hand had tightened on her chopsticks when I mentioned the woman at Piccolo's. The way she'd warned me to be careful about "connecting dots that might not connect."

The way she'd immediately started texting someone the moment she got in her car.

I thought about the letter signed "L." About Viola Lansing. About how she'd known Milo for years, bought his loyalty with her designs, understood his frustrations.

About how she'd been steering my investigation from the very beginning.

Maybe I had been seeing patterns that weren't there. Maybe paranoia and stress were making me suspicious of everyone.

Or maybe I was finally seeing clearly for the first time in forty years.

Back at the apartment, I changed into comfortable clothes and settled on the couch with Pippa. I pulled out my phone, meaning to back up more files to the cloud.

But as I scrolled through my notes, something caught my eye. The letter from Milo's apartment, signed with just the initial "L."

L for Lawrence Jung.

That's what I'd assumed. What everyone had assumed.

But what if it wasn't?

I thought about the woman at Piccolo's. Tall, slender, dark hair. Wearing sunglasses at night to hide her identity. Meeting with Ethan, arguing with him. "You promised me," he'd said.

Viola was tall and slender. She'd had dark hair for most of her life before going platinum blonde. She could have been wearing a wig.

And her last name was Lansing.

Viola Lansing.

L.

My heart started pounding. No. That was crazy. Viola wouldn't have met secretly with Ethan. She had no reason to.

Unless she did.

Unless there was something about their relationship I didn't know.

I sat there on my couch, staring at my phone, my mind spinning.

The way she'd been so interested in the investigation. The way she'd kept trying to steer my suspicions toward other people. The questions tonight about the woman at Piccolo's.

Was she trying to help me? Or was she trying to find out how much I knew?

I thought about dinner. About how genuine her concern had seemed.

But Viola had always been good at reading people, at knowing what to say, how to act. It was part of what made her successful in the fashion world.

What if she'd been playing me this whole time?

No. I was being paranoid again. Viola was my friend. My oldest friend.

Plus, Viola would have likely just signed "Vi" like she did on her cards and correspondence. She never used her last name with me.

But still, the L for Lansing nagged at me.

I looked at Pippa, who was watching me with concerned eyes.

"Am I crazy?" I whispered. "Am I seeing things that aren't there?"

She tilted her head but offered no answers.

I needed to know. I needed to find out if there was any connection between Viola and Ethan beyond what I knew.

But I had to be careful. Very careful.

Because if I was wrong, I'd be accusing my oldest friend of being involved in a murder.

And if I was right...

If I was right, then I'd been confiding in someone connected to a killer this whole time.

I pulled my computer onto my lap and started searching. Viola Lansing and Ethan Kemper. Any connection. Any mention of them together at events, in articles, anywhere.

It was going to be a long night.

Chapter Twenty-Three

By the time I closed the shop at five o'clock, I was exhausted. It had been a long day, made longer by the fact that I was still recovering from everything that had happened. My body ached in ways it hadn't in years, reminding me that I was, in fact, seventy-eight years old and not as resilient as I used to be.

"Come on, Pippa. Let's go home."

She hopped down from her window bed, stretching in that way dogs do, and trotted over to me. I clipped her leash to her collar and locked up the shop.

The walk back to the Royal Griffen felt longer than usual. My feet hurt, my back hurt, and all I wanted was to get home, make myself some tea, and spend the evening on my couch with Pippa.

Walter greeted us at the door with his usual smile. "Evening, Miss Dora Lee. Long day?"

"Very long. I'm getting too old for this."

"Nonsense. You're as spry as ever."

I laughed. "You're a terrible liar, Walter, but I appreciate it."

The lobby was quiet. Just a few residents coming and going, the usual evening routine. I headed to the elevator, Pippa at my side.

The doors opened and I stepped inside, pressing the button for the tenth floor. As the doors started to close, a hand shot out, stopping them.

Milo Savage stepped into the elevator.

My pulse quickened immediately. We were alone. Just the two of us in this small metal box. I pressed back against the wall, suddenly aware of how confined the space was. Four walls, no windows, nowhere to go.

"Miss Dora Lee," he said quietly. His eyes were red-rimmed, like he'd been crying. Or not sleeping. Or both. His clothes looked slept in, wrinkled.

"Milo."

The doors closed with a soft thud that felt too final. The elevator started to rise with its usual creaking groan.

For a moment, neither of us spoke. I watched the numbers light up above the door. Second floor. Third floor.

Milo stood perfectly still, staring at the doors. But I could see his reflection in the polished metal. His jaw was clenched, his hands opening and closing at his sides.

"Long day?" I asked, keeping my voice light, casual.

"Every day is long now." His voice was flat, exhausted. "Every single day."

Fourth floor.

"Are you alright, Milo? You look like you haven't been sleeping."

"I haven't." He turned slightly, and I could see his profile. Dark circles under his eyes. A muscle twitching in his jaw. "How do you sleep when you've done something you can't take back?"

My heart rate picked up, but I kept my breathing steady. "What do you mean?"

Fifth floor.

Then, suddenly, he reached out and slammed his hand against the emergency stop button.

The elevator jerked to a halt between the fifth and sixth floors. An alarm started blaring, loud and insistent in the confined space.

Pippa immediately started barking, her body tense, pressing against my legs.

"Milo, what are you doing?" I kept my voice calm, soothing. Like I was talking to a frightened animal. "Let's start the elevator again. We can talk while we ride."

"No." He shook his head violently. "If I wait, if we get to your floor, I'll lose my nerve. I need to say this now. I need to tell someone before I completely lose my mind."

"Then tell me. I'm listening."

He looked at me, and I saw desperation in his eyes. Raw, aching desperation. "You've been investigating. Asking questions everywhere. Talking to people, going to the hospital to see Jamie, showing up at presentations and fashion shows." His voice rose slightly. "You know, don't you? You know what I did."

"Why don't you tell me what you think I know?" I said gently, using the voice I'd perfected over decades of soothing nervous models backstage. "Start from the beginning."

He ran both hands through his hair, pulling at it. "We had another fight that day. Ethan told me he was bringing in a new business partner. Someone with better industry connections, better financial sense. He said I was..." His voice cracked. "He said I was dead weight. That anyone could do what I did."

"That must have hurt terribly."

"It destroyed me." The words came out in a whisper. "Everything I'd worked for, everything I'd built with him, he was just going to throw it away. Throw me away. Like I was nothing. Like I'd never mattered."

I stayed quiet, letting him continue. The alarm kept blaring, but he didn't seem to notice it anymore.

"So, I went for a run. To clear my head, to think, to figure out what to do." He was talking faster now, the words tumbling out. "But I couldn't stop thinking about it. About how he'd always done this. Always used people and threw them away when he was done with them. Used their ideas, their work, their talent, and then took all the credit."

"You came back early," I prompted softly.

"I came back." He nodded, his movements jerky. "I used the maintenance keycard I'd taken from the supply closet weeks ago. Got in through the service entrance where no one would see me. Where Walter wouldn't mark me down in his log."

"And Ethan was in the gym."

"He was about to go into the sauna. We argued again. Worse than before." Tears started streaming down his face. "He said I was replaceable. That I should be grateful he'd even let me be part of his success. Like I hadn't designed half the pieces in that collection. Like I hadn't handled every business detail while he played the creative genius."

The elevator alarm continued its shrill cry. Someone would come soon. They had to.

"What happened next, Milo?"

"I knew he'd been taking pills. Amphetamines. He took them to stay thin, to have energy for the long days. Everyone who worked with him knew, but nobody talked about it." His hands clenched into fists. "I knew they'd make the heat worse. Make it harder for his body to regulate temperature. Make his heart race."

"So, you pushed him inside."

"I pushed him inside the sauna." The confession came out in a rush now, like he couldn't hold it back anymore. "And I jammed a crowbar through the door handle. I told myself I just wanted to scare him. Make him understand how it felt to be trapped, to be powerless. But then I heard him pounding on the door, yelling, begging me to let him out, and I just... I stood there. I stood there and I let him die."

My chest tightened. Even though I'd suspected, hearing him say it out loud in this trapped metal box made it real in a way it hadn't been before.

"Milo, you need to turn yourself in," I said gently. "Tell the police what you told me. They'll understand—"

"There's more." He wiped his face with the back of his hand. "Jamie. The model who used to work for Ethan. I saw her at the memorial, leaving flowers, and I thought... I thought maybe she'd seen something that day. Or maybe she knew something. She'd been watching the building, following Ethan's schedule."

"So, you followed her."

"I borrowed a car. Waited for her near her apartment." His voice dropped to barely a whisper. "I just wanted to scare her. That's all. Just scare her enough that she'd stop asking questions, stop talking about Ethan. I saw her step off the curb and I just... I aimed the car at her. I told myself I'd swerve away at the last second, but I didn't. I hit her. I heard the impact and I just kept driving."

"She's recovering," I said quietly. "She's going to be okay."

"Is she?" His eyes searched mine desperately. "Is she really? Because I've been thinking about her every day, wondering if I killed her too, if I've got two murders on my conscience instead of one."

"Milo, listen to me. You need to—"

"I can't!" His voice cracked, rising to nearly a shout. "Don't you see? I've already tried to stop this. I broke into your apartment. That was me."

My blood ran cold. "You destroyed my home."

"I had to! You had evidence, notes, photos. I found them. I took everything and destroyed it." His eyes were wild now, desperate. "But it doesn't matter, does it? You remember it all. You saw everything. You're going to tell them."

"The police already know most of this," I said, keeping my voice calm even as fear started to claw at my chest. "Detective Keller has seen evidence. She's building a case. Turning yourself in now, cooperating, that's your best option."

"Then it's already too late." The desperation in his voice shifted to something darker. "If they already know, if you've already told them, then I've got nothing left to lose."

"You have your life, Milo. You're young. Even with—"

"You can't testify against me." He grabbed my shoulders, his grip tight enough to hurt. "Please, Miss Dora Lee. I'm begging you. Just forget this conversation. Forget everything."

Pippa launched herself at him, barking furiously, but he shook her off.

"Milo, you're not thinking clearly." I tried to keep my voice steady, tried to use the cunning that had served me well for seventy-eight years. "Hurting me won't help you. It'll only make things worse."

"I know." His voice cracked. "I know, but I can't... I can't go to prison. I can't spend the rest of my life locked up for this."

His hands moved to my throat.

Time seemed to slow down. I looked into his eyes and saw the desperation there, the fear, the terrible resolve of someone who had nothing left to lose.

This was it. I was going to die in this elevator. The same building where I'd lived my entire life, where I'd played as a child, where I'd hidden in dumbwaiters and spied on guests. Where I'd built my career, my life, my home.

And now it would end here, in this metal box between floors, at the hands of a desperate young man who'd made terrible choices.

I thought of Pippa, who would be left alone. Of Georgie and Chelsea and Walter and Jerry, who'd become my family. Of Viola, my oldest friend, who I'd doubted.

Of all the clothes I'd never make, the colors I'd never blend, the runway shows I'd never see.

But then something else rose up inside me. Not fear, but anger.

Determination.

I hadn't survived seventy-eight years, hadn't built a career from nothing, hadn't lived through decades of ups and downs in the cutthroat fashion industry, just to die like this.

Not today.

I brought my knee up as hard as I could.

Milo gasped and stumbled backward, his hands leaving my throat.

Pippa, sensing her moment, sank her teeth into his leg with a fierce growl I'd never heard from her before.

"Get off!" Milo screamed, trying to shake her loose. "Get off me!"

I lunged for the emergency stop button, slamming my hand against it. The elevator lurched back into motion with a grinding sound.

"I'm sorry!" Milo was crying now, still trying to dislodge Pippa. "I'm so sorry. I didn't mean to. I didn't mean for any of this to happen."

The elevator dinged. Fifth floor. Sixth floor.

"You had a choice," I said, my voice hoarse. "Every step of the way, you had a choice."

Seventh floor. Eighth floor.

"Lawrence said it would be better. He said I deserved more. He said—" Milo's voice was frantic now, words tumbling out. "He kept talking about how Ethan held me back, how I'd never be anything while Ethan was around. He made it sound so reasonable, so logical."

Ninth floor.

"Lawrence manipulated you," I said. "But you're the one who made the final choice."

The elevator dinged again. Tenth floor.

The doors opened.

And there, in the hallway, was half the building staff. Walter, Chelsea, Jerry. They must have been called when the emergency alarm went off.

"Call the police!" I shouted, my voice raw. "Now!"

Milo finally shook Pippa free and tried to push past me, but Walter moved with surprising speed for a man his age, grabbing Milo's arm.

"I don't think so, son."

Jerry appeared on Milo's other side, and together they held him while Chelsea already had her phone out, speaking rapidly to 911.

Milo collapsed between them, sobbing. "I'm sorry. I'm so sorry. I didn't mean to kill him. I didn't want any of this to happen."

I scooped up Pippa, who was still growling at Milo, and held her close. My hands were shaking. My whole body was shaking.

"It's okay, girl," I whispered into her fur. "You did good. Such a good girl."

Within minutes, sirens filled the air. Detective Keller arrived with several other officers, and they took Milo into custody. He didn't resist. Just kept crying, kept apologizing, kept saying he was sorry.

Detective Keller came over to me, her expression grim. "Miss Griffen, are you alright? Did he hurt you?"

I touched my throat. It was sore, but not seriously injured. "No. Pippa protected me."

She looked down at my dog with new respect. "Good dog." Then to me: "I need you to tell me exactly what happened."

I told her everything. The confession, how he'd known about Ethan's amphetamine use and used it against him, how he'd jammed the sauna door with a crowbar, how he'd admitted to breaking into my apartment and destroying my evidence, how he'd deliberately hit Jamie with a car trying to scare or silence her, how he'd been manipulated by Lawrence Jung, how he'd panicked when he realized I could testify against him, the attack. She recorded it all, taking notes, asking clarifying questions.

"We've been building the case against him," she said when I finished. "Your evidence helped enormously. But a confession..." She shook her head. "That seals it. He'll go away for a long time."

"What about Lawrence Jung?"

"We'll bring him in for questioning. If we can prove he knowingly encouraged Milo to commit murder, we can charge him with conspiracy." She closed her notebook. "But that's harder to prove."

After she finished taking my statement, Georgie appeared, having been called by Chelsea.

"Miss Dora Lee, honey, let me take you inside. You've had enough excitement for one day."

I didn't argue. I was shaking, the adrenaline finally wearing off, leaving me feeling weak and ancient.

Georgie helped me into my apartment, Pippa still in my arms. Once inside, she made me sit down and brought me water and a blanket, wrapping it around my shoulders like I was a child.

"You just rest. I'm going to stay here tonight. You shouldn't be alone."

"You don't have to—"

"I'm staying. End of discussion." Her voice was firm but kind. "Besides, someone needs to make sure that brave little dog gets extra treats."

As if on cue, Pippa's tail wagged.

Walter knocked on the still-open door, holding a steaming mug. "I made you some tea, Miss Dora Lee. With honey, the way you like it."

"Thank you, Walter."

He set it on the table beside me, his weathered face creased with concern. "That was a brave thing you did. Talking to him like that, keeping calm."

"I was terrified."

"Brave doesn't mean not being scared. It means being scared and doing it anyway." He patted my hand gently. "You rest now. We'll all be keeping extra watch tonight."

After he left, Chelsea appeared with a plate of cookies from the lobby's coffee station.

"Thought you might need something sweet after all that."

"You're all too good to me."

"You're family, Miss Dora Lee. That's what family does."

Jerry showed up an hour later, even though he should have been sleeping before his night shift.

"Just wanted to check on you. Make sure you're okay."

I looked around at all of them. Georgie sitting in my armchair, keeping watch like a guardian. Chelsea on her phone, probably rearranging tomorrow's schedule so she could check on me more often. Walter popping back in every twenty minutes with some new offering: more tea, a sandwich, a warm compress for the bruises forming on my shoulders.

And Jerry, who should be sleeping, standing in my doorway with genuine concern on his tired face.

"I'm okay," I said, and for the first time in days, I actually meant it. "Thanks to all of you."

They stayed for another hour, keeping me company, making sure I ate something, checking that my door was properly locked before they finally left. Georgie was the last to go, only after I promised I'd call her if I needed anything, anything at all.

"And I mean it, Miss Dora Lee. You call me at three in the morning if you need to. I'll come right over."

After she left, I sat on my couch with Pippa, wrapped in my blanket, drinking the last of the tea Walter had brought.

It was over. The mystery was solved. Ethan's killer had confessed and been arrested.

But something still nagged at me.

Milo had mentioned Lawrence, how Lawrence had manipulated him, encouraged him, made it all sound reasonable. Lawrence who'd swooped in immediately after Ethan's death. Lawrence who was now in control of the brand.

Lawrence who would probably walk away from this relatively unscathed, having gotten exactly what he wanted without having to actually commit murder himself.

The fashion industry was ruthless indeed.

But there was something else. Something about the way Milo had talked about Lawrence. The way he'd said "Lawrence kept talking about how Ethan held me back."

Who had been talking to Lawrence? Who had put the idea in his head?

I thought about Viola. About her warnings, her interest in the investigation, her questions.

About how she'd tried so hard to steer suspicion toward Jamie.

About the letter signed "L."

No. I was being paranoid. Viola was my friend.

But that seed of doubt, once planted, was hard to ignore.

I looked at Pippa, who was watching me with her big, concerned eyes.

"What do you think, girl? Am I seeing patterns that aren't there?"

She tilted her head, ears flopping, but offered no answers.

Tomorrow, I would think about it more. Tomorrow, I would decide what to do with these suspicions.

But tonight, I was just grateful to be alive. Grateful for Pippa, who'd saved me. Grateful for this found family who'd rallied around me.

Grateful that, at seventy-eight years old, I still had fight left in me.

I pulled Pippa close and closed my eyes, finally allowing myself to rest.

It was over.

Or at least, this part was.

Chapter Twenty-Four

The first few days after Milo's arrest were a blur.

I slept a lot, more than I had in years. My body had finally given me permission to rest, and I took it. Georgie stayed over the first two nights, insisting she wasn't leaving me alone. Chelsea took the third night, bringing a sleeping bag and camping out on my newly repaired couch.

"You don't have to do this," I told them repeatedly.

"We know," they both said. "We're doing it anyway."

Walter had taken to walking me to the shop each morning, even though it was only a block and a half away. He'd wait until I had the door unlocked and the lights on before heading back to his post.

"Just making sure you get there safe, Miss Dora Lee."

And Jerry, who normally slept during the day after his night shifts, had started stopping by my apartment each evening around six to check on me.

"Just wanted to see if you needed anything. Groceries? Light bulbs? Someone to complain to?"

They'd all become my family. Not just building staff, but true family.

By the fourth day, I insisted I was fine on my own.

"I can't have you all losing sleep over me forever. I'm okay. Really."

Reluctantly, they agreed. But I knew they were all keeping extra watch, checking in more often than usual.

Detective Keller stopped by that same afternoon with an update.

"Milo Savage has been formally charged with murder in the first degree. He's confessed everything, cooperating fully. His lawyer is trying to work out a plea deal, but given the premeditation..." She shook her head. "He's looking at twenty-five to life."

"What about Lawrence Jung?"

"We brought him in for questioning. He admitted to talking with Milo about taking over the brand, but claims he had no knowledge that Milo was planning to kill Ethan. Says it was all business talk, hypothetical." She sighed. "Without concrete evidence that he encouraged or knew about the murder, we can't charge him. He's been cleared."

"So, he just walks away?"

"For now. But we'll be keeping an eye on him." She closed her notebook. "The fashion industry has a way of taking care of its own problems. Word's already spreading about his connection to this case. His reputation is taking a hit."

After she left, I sat with that information. Lawrence had manipulated Milo, pushed him toward murder, and now walked away free. It didn't sit right with me, but sometimes that's how justice worked.

Or didn't work.

A week after the arrest, I was at the shop when Jamie stopped by. She'd been checking on me daily, either by phone or in person. Today she had coffee and pastries from a nearby bakery.

"Thought you might need a mid-morning pick-me-up."

"You're an angel."

We sat in the shop, Pippa begging shamelessly for bits of croissant, while we talked.

"How are you really doing?" Jamie asked.

"Better. Still processing everything, but better."

"I can't believe it was Milo all along. And that he actually confessed to you in an elevator." She shuddered. "That must have been terrifying."

"It was. But Pippa saved me." I scratched behind Pippa's ears, and she leaned into my hand happily.

"She's a hero." Jamie smiled at my dog, then looked at me with a more serious expression. "Miss Dora Lee, remember when I was in the hospital and you said you might have something for me?"

I thought back to that conversation. Jamie lying in her hospital bed, bruised and broken, worried that her career was over. "I remember."

"I didn't bring it up after you got out of the hospital because you had a lot going on, but..." She took a breath. "I'm ready for whatever you have in mind."

I looked at her. She'd healed well, the bruises faded, the cast off her arm. But more than that, there was a strength in her eyes that hadn't been there before. A determination.

"What if we did a runway show?" I said.

Her eyes widened. "A runway show?"

"My work. A comeback collection. Something that shows the industry that quality and craftsmanship still matter." I stood up and started pulling pieces from the racks. "Look at this. And this. Bold colors, vintage-inspired silhouettes, hand-sewn details. Everything the industry claims to want but rarely actually supports."

Jamie jumped up, examining the pieces I'd pulled. "This is incredible. These colors, these patterns..." She held up a dress in a vibrant geometric print. "People would go crazy for this. The fashion blogs alone would eat it up."

"You really think so?"

"I know so. I work in this industry, remember? I see what's trending, what buyers are looking for." She turned to face me, excitement building in her voice. "We could do something intimate but impactful. Invite the right people, get some press coverage. Show everyone that Dora Lee Griffen is back."

"It would take a lot of work."

"I'll help. I know people, venues, models who would love to walk for you. We could call it..." She paused, thinking. "What about 'All the Rage?' Because your work used to be all the rage, and it's going to be again."

"All the Rage," I repeated, testing it out. "I like it."

"So, you'll do it?"

I looked around at my shop. At the racks of dresses, the displays of jackets and skirts, the fabric waiting to be transformed into something beautiful. At Pippa in her window bed, and at Jamie standing there with hopeful, excited eyes.

"Yes," I said. "Let's do it."

Jamie squealed and hugged me. "This is going to be amazing! I'll start making calls right now. We need a venue, a date, models, hair and makeup—"

"Jamie, breathe. We have time to plan this properly."

"Right. Right. Proper planning." She laughed. "I'm just so excited. This is going to be incredible, Miss Dora Lee. You're going to remind everyone why you're a legend."

After Jamie left, buzzing with plans and ideas, I sat at my workbench and pulled out my laptop. Something was still nagging at me. That letter signed "L." The woman at Piccolo's wearing sunglasses at night.

Viola Lansing.

I typed "Viola Lansing Ethan Kemper" into the search bar.

The results were sparse. A few mentions of them both attending the same industry events over the years. A photo from a runway show five years ago where they were both in the audience, though not sitting together. An article about up-and-coming designers that mentioned Ethan in passing, with Viola quoted as one of the established designers commenting on the new generation.

Nothing suspicious. Nothing that suggested they'd had any relationship beyond normal industry acquaintanceship.

But that didn't mean there wasn't one. It just meant they'd been careful.

I tried different search terms. "Viola Lansing menswear Ethan Kemper." "Viola Lansing Piccolo's restaurant." "Viola Lansing Lawrence Jung."

Nothing.

I sat back, staring at the screen, frustration building in my chest. This was the problem with people like Viola. Forty years in the fashion industry had taught her how to work in the shadows. How to make connections without leaving traces. How to manipulate situations without getting her hands dirty.

If she had been involved, she wouldn't have left an obvious paper trail.

I thought about the woman at Piccolo's. Wearing sunglasses at night. Meeting Ethan in secret. Arguing with him about a broken promise.

Marco had said she was tall, slender, dark-haired, sophisticated. Expensive taste.

That was Viola. Or it could have been.

But "could have been" wasn't proof. It was just suspicion. And suspicion without evidence was just paranoia.

I pulled up photos of Viola from five years ago, before she went platinum. There was her natural dark brown, almost black hair. The same hair color Marco had described.

But lots of women had dark hair. Lots of women were tall and slender. Lots of women in the fashion industry had sophisticated taste.

I tried searching for any connection between Viola and Milo beyond the obvious customer relationship. Articles mentioning them together. Events they'd both attended. Any indication that their relationship was more than just designer and loyal customer.

Nothing concrete. Just the fact that Milo wore her designs exclusively. That he'd bought from her for years. That she'd mentioned knowing him, understanding his frustrations.

Which could mean everything. Or nothing.

I thought about the letter signed "L." If it was from Lawrence Jung, why hide behind an initial? Lawrence had no reason to be secretive. He was ambitious, ruthless, but not subtle. He'd moved in on the brand openly, publicly.

But if the letter was from Viola Lansing, secrecy made perfect sense. She'd spent forty years building a reputation. She couldn't afford to be connected to a murder, not even tangentially.

I sat there, staring at the screen, my mind going in circles.

All I had were pieces that might fit together. Or might not.

The woman at Piccolo's who could have been Viola.

The letter signed "L" that could have been from Lansing.

The way Viola had steered my investigation from the beginning.

The way she'd pushed suspicion toward Jamie.

The way she'd warned me, over and over, to stop investigating.

The way her hand had tightened on her chopsticks at dinner when I described the woman at Piccolo's.

The way she'd immediately started texting someone when she left the restaurant.

But none of it was proof. None of it would hold up in court. None of it would convince Detective Keller or anyone else.

It was just the instinct of someone who'd spent seventy-eight years reading people. Who'd built a career on noticing details others missed. Who'd survived in the cutthroat fashion industry by understanding when someone was lying.

And my instincts were screaming that Viola was hiding something.

But maybe that's all they were. Instincts. Paranoia. The suspicions of an exhausted old woman who'd been through too much and was seeing threats everywhere.

I closed the laptop with more force than necessary. Pippa's head popped up from her bed, looking at me with concern.

"I don't know, girl," I said, running a hand through my hair. "I don't know if I'm being smart or if I'm losing my mind."

She came over and pressed against my legs, offering silent comfort.

The frustrating thing was that I'd probably never know for sure. Milo was going to prison. Lawrence had been cleared. The case was closed as far as the police were concerned.

If Viola had been involved, if she'd been pulling strings, manipulating people, encouraging Milo's resentment, she'd done it carefully enough that there was no evidence. No trail. No proof.

Just a seventy-eight-year-old woman's suspicions about her oldest friend.

And what kind of friend suspects someone of murder based on nothing but gut feeling?

That evening, as I was putting away my laptop, my phone rang.

Viola.

I answered, and before I could say hello, she spoke.

"There you are! You actually sound like yourself today. Every time I've called this week, you've been so exhausted I didn't want to keep you on the phone long."

She had called. I remembered now, brief conversations where she'd asked how I was, if I needed anything, but I'd been too tired to talk much.

"I am feeling better. Getting back to normal."

"Good. I've been so worried about you, Dora Lee. When I first heard what happened with Milo Savage, that he attacked you in that elevator..." Her voice was warm with genuine concern. "I still can't believe it. Being trapped with him, knowing what he'd done."

"It was frightening. But it's over now."

"Is it though?" She paused. "I heard Lawrence Jung was questioned but they let him go. He manipulated that poor boy into murder and he's just... free."

"The police couldn't prove he knew about the murder beforehand."

"The police can't prove a lot of things. Doesn't mean they didn't happen." There was an edge to her voice that I couldn't quite read. "Lawrence Jung is a snake, Dora Lee. Always has been. Be careful around him."

Was she warning me about Lawrence? Or deflecting attention away from herself?

I pushed the thought away. This was exactly the kind of paranoid thinking that had consumed me for the past hour.

"I don't plan to be around him at all."

"Good. Stay away from that whole mess." She softened. "Listen, I know things have been strained between us lately. I've been worried about you, pushing you to stop investigating, and maybe I came on too strong. I just... I care about you. You're one of my oldest friends, and I don't want to lose you."

The guilt intensified. "You're not going to lose me, Vi."

"I'm glad to hear that. How about dinner next week? My treat. We can celebrate you surviving all of this."

"That sounds nice."

"Good. I'll call you in a few days and we'll set it up." She paused. "Oh, and Dora Lee? I heard through the grapevine that you're planning a comeback show. 'All the Rage,' they're calling it?"

"Word travels fast."

"It always does in this industry. I think it's wonderful. You're going to show all these young designers what real fashion looks like."

After we hung up, I sat there with my phone in my hand, trying to sort through what I felt.

Viola had been exactly what she'd always been: concerned, caring, supportive. My friend.

Or she'd been exactly what she'd always been: calculating, strategic, always three steps ahead. My rival.

After forty years, I still couldn't tell which was true. Maybe both were. Maybe that's what made us such good friends. Or such perfect frenemies.

The paranoia and stress had made me see shadows everywhere. Question everyone. Even the people closest to me.

But somewhere deep down, that tiny voice still whispered: but what if?

What if Viola had been the woman at Piccolo's? What if she'd made promises to Ethan she hadn't kept? What if she'd encouraged Milo's resentment, pushed him toward murder, and then stepped back to let him take the fall?

What if my oldest friend had been playing chess with people's lives, and I'd been too close to see it?

I pushed the thoughts away. I was done investigating. Done suspecting everyone around me. Milo had killed Ethan, and he was going to pay for it.

That was justice enough.

It had to be.

Because the alternative, that Viola had been manipulating all of us and I couldn't prove it, was too frustrating to accept.

The next morning, I woke up early and went straight to my workbench. If I was going to do this runway show, I needed to start creating. I pulled out my sketchpad and began drawing, my hand moving across the page with a confidence I hadn't felt in years.

Bold silhouettes. Vibrant colors. Textures and patterns that would make people stop and stare.

Pippa watched me from her bed, her head tilted, ears flopping.

"What do you think, girl? Should we show them what we're made of?"

She stood up, stretched, and trotted over to me. I expected her to beg for breakfast, but instead she did something she hadn't done since she was a puppy.

She placed both paws on my knee and looked up at me with those enormous eyes, tail wagging slowly. Then she did her signature move, the one I'd taught her years ago: a little bow, front legs stretched out, back end in the air.

"Are you telling me to take a bow?" I laughed. "We haven't even done the show yet."

She barked once, then did it again. Her bow.

"You're right. We're going to knock them dead." I scratched behind her ridiculous ears. "Figuratively speaking, of course. We've had enough actual death around here."

She spun in a circle, then sat down and offered me her paw.

I shook it solemnly. "It's a deal, Miss Pippa. You and me. We're doing this."

I spent the rest of the morning sketching and pulling pieces from my inventory that could work for the show. Some would need alterations, some were perfect as they were. I'd need to create at least ten new pieces to round out the collection, maybe fifteen.

It was ambitious. Maybe too ambitious for a seventy-eight-year-old woman who'd just survived a murder investigation and an attack in an elevator.

But as I worked, feeling the familiar flow of creativity, I knew I could do it.

I'd built a career from nothing once before. I could do it again.

Around noon, there was a knock at the door. I opened it to find Walter holding a newspaper.

"Thought you might want to see this, Miss Dora Lee."

He handed me the fashion section. There, in a small article near the back, was a headline: "Fashion Legend Dora Lee Griffen Announces Comeback Show."

I skimmed the article. It talked about my history in the industry, my disappearance from the scene, and now my return with "All the Rage," described as an intimate showcase of her signature bold colors and vintage-inspired silhouettes.

"How did they even know about this?" I asked. "We just decided yesterday."

Walter grinned. "That Jamie girl has been busy. She's been talking to everyone, drumming up interest. Smart one, that girl."

"She certainly is."

"The building's proud of you, Miss Dora Lee. Showing those young folks that age is just a number."

After he left, I looked at the article again. There was a small photo of me from decades ago, standing beside one of my runway pieces. I barely recognized that young woman with dark hair and a confident smile.

But maybe she was still in there somewhere. Maybe this show would prove it.

I went back to my workbench and kept sketching. Pippa settled at my feet, content to just be near me.

By evening, I had fifteen sketches completed. Fifteen pieces that told a story of color, creativity, and craftsmanship. Pieces that said: I'm still here. I still matter. I still have something to say.

Jamie called just as I was finishing the last sketch.

"Have you seen the article? It's everywhere on social media. People are so excited!"

"I saw it. You work fast."

"We need to strike while the iron's hot. I've already got three venues interested, and I have a list of models who want to walk. This is really happening, Miss Dora Lee!"

Her enthusiasm was infectious. "When are you thinking?"

"Two months? That gives us time to finish the collection and promote properly."

"Two months. I can do that."

"You absolutely can. I'll come by tomorrow and we'll start planning everything." She paused. "Thank you for giving me this chance. After everything that happened, after everyone writing me off, you believed in me."

"You believed in yourself first. That's what matters."

After we hung up, I looked around my apartment. At the sketches spread across my workbench. At Pippa sleeping peacefully. At the view of the city through my window, the same view I'd had my entire life.

I was seventy-eight years old. I'd survived a murder investigation. I'd been attacked and nearly killed. I'd doubted my oldest friend and felt guilty about it.

But I was still here. Still creating. Still dreaming.

And for the first time in a very long time, I felt hope.

Hope for my career. Hope for my future. Hope that maybe, just maybe, the best was still ahead of me.

I picked up Pippa and carried her to the couch, settling in with her warm weight against me.

"What do you think, girl? One more adventure?"

She licked my hand and snuggled closer.

"Yeah. Me too."

Outside my window, the city lights twinkled against the darkening sky. Somewhere out there, people were designing, creating, dreaming. And now, I was one of them again.

The mystery was solved. The killer was caught. Justice had been served.

But my story? My story was just beginning again.

THE END

Before you go: If you loved Haute Mess, be sure to visit my website to sign up for my newsletter (if you haven't already) and to stay up to date on new releases and other bookish things.

Also, check out my other books! You can find links on my website.

www.ejwheltonwrites.com

Author note:

I bought a set of book covers on a whim. I saw it and instantly knew the character, knew her story, and wanted to tell the world.

That character was Dora Lee Griffen and her dog Pippa. She's a feisty lady with street smarts and a dark sense of humor. Loves to play the "sweet, innocent old lady" bit. It gets her access to information and places she has no business being.

I hope you did enjoy meeting Dora Lee because I have five more books planned with her and Pippa. Along the way, she changes and finds "family" that she never knew she wanted.

www.ejwheltonwrites.com